MW00628382

INTO
TERRIBLE
LIGHT

INTO TERRIBLE LIGHT

DAVID RUTSCHMAN

FORKLIFT_BOOKS

FORKLIFT BOOKS EDITION, SEPTEMBER 2017

ISBN 978-0-9995931-4-1

Edited by Matt Hart
Book design and cover photo by Eric Appleby
Author photo by Sara Tashker

Cincinnati, Ohio

WWW.FORKLIFTBOOKS.COM

CONTENTS

ONE

TWO

THREE

FOUR

FIVE

The answer is there, the answer is there
but there
is not a fixed position

—Fugazi

Consider whether any being or any world
could ever be excluded from right now

—Eihei Dogen

INTO
TERRIBLE
LIGHT

ONE

FATHERHOOD

I was teaching my son to throw stones into the water when he became a stone and I threw him in the water.

"My boy, my darling boy," I called and I hurled myself after him and I became a stone and we tumbled down to the silent muddy bottom.

We were together then, two smooth stones.

"Terrorists?" he asked.

"Yeah," I said.

"And cancer?" he asked.

"Yeah," I said.

"And the decline of turtle populations, and the skies filled with bombs?" he asked and I said, "Yeah, I know, I know, of course, but—"

"What will become of us?" he cried and I said, "We'll be all right, I think," and tried to explain something about courage and tenderness and human dignity, but he was not reassured. A fish flashed above us in the murky water, its belly a streak of silver.

"Can you keep me safe?" he asked quietly, and I hesitated just a beat before I said "Yes," and by then he was already onto me—my sharp kid—and though I tried and tried, I could not reach out to him, being a stone.

MOST OF US AROUND HERE

Most of us around here are like *this*, but there are some—a few—who are like *that*.

It's confusing. It makes us a little uncomfortable.

I mean, acceptance and all, for sure, but still.

There are more of them in town now than there used to be, for one thing. And we're concerned, honestly. Don't we have a right?

Because we've heard that some of them who are like *that* were once like *this* themselves. Which raises questions.

About our own families, for example, our friends and neighbors. If some of them?

Or even we ourselves?

Although of course not.

Unless that's what they thought too, those who are like *that*. Formerly.

Back when they were still like *this*.

STORY

When she was a little girl she drove with her parents across New Mexico. The land went on forever, huge and arid and stark, skinny trees bent by the wind, dry earth, yellow grasses. She remembers passing a pickup with some children in the back and remembers that the other kids didn't acknowledge her in the car with her parents, didn't wave or nod, but stayed staring straight ahead.

The girl and her parents were driving back to the Midwest after visiting relatives in California, and the father, trying to take a shortcut he found on the map, got lost. Just like that they found themselves on a dirt road through a plain, with evening coming on, and as they crested a slight rise they suddenly scared three antelope that were grazing not far away. The antelope jerked into a gallop as the car came alongside. They ran, all three. And somehow in their confusion they ran, not *away* from the road, but parallel to it—only a few feet from the car and a few feet ahead. Swift, graceful creatures. The girl pressed her face to the window.

How fast are they going? the mother asked, and the father, looking at the speedometer, whistled and said forty-five. He was driving with only one hand, the girl noticed.

She saw the fence from a long way off. It was barbed wire, strung tight on cedar posts. No one spoke. The father didn't slow down, and later the girl, remembering this, would wonder why he hadn't eased up on the gas, let the antelope drop down to a trot, but he must not have realized.

The animals hit the fence in a cloud of dust and hooves and rolling bodies. One of them slid and scrambled beneath the lowest wire and righted itself and kept galloping, alone now, across the plain at an angle. The other two had their necks snapped back, and fell and rolled in the dirt, and then the car was past them, roaring forward.

Her father swallowed and put his other hand on the steering wheel. Her mother reached over and touched his arm. They were driving on. The entire thing had taken less than a minute.

In the beginning, the girl understood this story about the antelope to be simply an account of something she had witnessed—and she told it in that way, on the rare occasions when she told it.

But as the years went by and the girl, a woman now, started to see some friends of hers succeed in the world in ways that she couldn't, she began to think that the story was about what it is to be galloping forward in a group, and be suddenly brought up short, and watch someone who had been beside you the moment before sprint on without you. And, for herself at least, and the people closest to her, she used the story to illustrate this feeling, to explain it.

At least until the summer her parents died . . . her mother first, her father . . . and the meaning of the story changed for her. The nights were oven-hot, humid. Lying in bed, she remembered the three antelope and the three people in the car and she thought that the story was about running forward in a group, and finding yourself alone—still moving, still charging ahead, but now without the others. The others cut down. The sheets were tangled, damp with her sweat.

After the birth of her own daughter, though, she began to worry about the story . . . maybe both of her interpretations had been wrong. Maybe the story was only a description. Wasn't this how she had told it at first? Antelope galloping into a fence? Their lean bodies. Just something that had happened once . . . years before . . . that she had seen with her very own eyes. Those churning legs, that sky. Her daughter reached up and grabbed her by the cheek. Maybe it didn't mean anything. The barbed wire waiting.

THE HOGS, THE SOW, THE WIND

1. Once there were two hogs and a sow . . .

Once there were two hogs and a sow who lived in a sturdy pen outside an old man's hut. Then the old man died. That morning, no one brought food to the pen; the next morning, no one brought food to the pen. By evening the animals were panicked and ravenous, the bottom of the trough licked smooth as tile. "The man will come with food tomorrow," one hog assured the rest. "He always comes with food."

"Well, he didn't come today, smart guy," the other hog snapped back, his voice rising. "So watch it with that *always*." For a long moment they glowered at each other, but then the sow intervened.

"Hey," she said sharply. "Hey, come on." The hunger was a swelling inside of her.

Each made a silent decision to let the tension dissipate. They were siblings, the three of them. They were so hungry.

In one corner of the pen stood their water container: a half barrel of rainwater. They filled their bellies with water and spent a restless night. The next morning, again, no one brought food.

"Why isn't he bringing food?" the first hog asked over and over. "He always brings food." It had never occurred to any of them that one day there might not be food. With food, everything else had clicked into place: sky and pen, the grunting of the other pigs, the wheel of days and seasons. But without food, all the familiar objects of their life became unrecognizable somehow, though also precisely the same. The trough, the clouds overhead. Without food, the ground disappeared, and there was only falling, or a feeling just like falling.

"We've got to make a plan. We've got to break out." The first hog was frantic, near tears. "It's the only way."

"Maybe he'll come tomorrow?" said the second hog.

"I'm telling you, we have to find a way out and go, go, go." The first hog paced from one end of the pen to the other.

The sow shook her head as if to clear her vision. "What do you mean, find a way out? There is no way out." She went to the rain barrel and lapped more water.

"He always brings food," the first hog said again. "Why isn't he bringing food?"

Over the next few days they came to realize that escape was their only choice. But how could they break free of the pen? Though they spent hours inspecting every inch of the strong wooden slats, they could find no exit.

The hunger turned from an ache, to a fire, to a weakness inside of them. They were dizzy with it. It turned from a weakness back into a fire while they combed the pen for a gap.

At last they came up with a solution: If they were to knock the rain barrel over and hoist it into the trough, maybe one of them could stand with both front legs on the barrel. Another one, then, could climb unsteadily onto the first animal's back, and if this one could reach the top of the fence, the remaining sibling could clamber over them both and drop to the other side.

The plan was a good one, except that the two who used their bodies in this way would be left inside the pen to die. "That's the only flaw," the first hog said, nodding, and when the others snorted and laughed, he laughed, too, a sound that was close to tears in its rawness.

"The only flaw!" the second hog repeated. "You think?" Again they erupted in laughter.

It took them some time to compose themselves. "Just a flaw for two of us," the sow said after they had been quiet for a minute. A feeling of closeness had developed while they were laughing together, but the sow's words put an end to that.

What choice did they have? They decided to draw lots for who would stay and who would go. Before the drawing, they walked the pen one last time, inspecting the strong boards.

"It's the only way," one said.

They gathered three pebbles: two light gray, one dark.

"Here we go," the sow whispered.

At the count of three, they closed their eyes. Each selected a pebble. They looked at the pebbles and at each other. The outcome was clear: the sow and the first hog would make a ramp of their bodies with the trough and the rain barrel, and the second hog would climb to freedom. The chosen hog felt the victory thrill through him, the sweet relief, though he did his best to hide it. The hunger had turned into a claw. Soon he would be outside the pen. No one spoke.

But then the hog who had been selected to stay behind and make a ramp with his body began to shake his head. "No," he said. "No you don't!" he yelled. He said he refused to starve and die. He accused the others of cheating. He turned his back on them and stood trembling in the corner of the pen. "No!" he shouted.

"Fair's fair," said the one who'd been selected to escape.

"What do you mean, 'No'?" said the sow.

But the hog wouldn't hear it. "No," he said again. "No, no, no." He snarled at them. "Cheaters! Trying to cheat." His face was hard to look at. Inside him the hunger had turned into an avalanche. It was sliding.

"We didn't cheat," the other hog said.

"How could we have cheated?" the sow asked.

But he wouldn't hear it. "Draw again," he insisted. "Cheaters."

Over the next few hours they circled each other, shouting. Before too long the sow had taken sides with the refusing hog, and the two of them tried to convince their brother to draw again. "If he thinks we cheated, we owe it to him to do it over," the sow said to the hog who had thought he would be free. Her voice was sugary and crafty and pained. "Just to make it all above reproach."

The chosen hog hollered and argued. He briefly had the sensation that he was no longer a hog who was hungry, but rather a hunger in the shape of a hog. He shook his head back and forth and muttered. He remembered the thrill when he'd seen the pebble. Finally he saw that he had no choice.

"OK," he said. "Let's draw again."

The sow felt the hunger subside in a rush, replaced by a kind of joy and a kind of cunning. This time the pebble would be hers.

The refusing hog could find no words for what was inside him. There was something that had been hunger, and something that had been terror, and something else like a strong wind blowing. It took him a long time to understand that his brother and sister had agreed to draw again.

In silence they returned to the trough. It was well past midday now: flat, hot sky.

In silence they chose their pebbles.

Now it was the sow who would go free. The hog who had been selected the first time felt himself reel. He couldn't find his feet.

The sow was making a high-pitched noise, like a keening. It was partly a celebration, but only partly. Inside her the hunger had become a shining light. It was so bright she could see only the pebble. "Let's go, guys," she said, her words edging around the light. "Let's make the ramp."

The refusing hog, the one who had called them both cheaters, was backing away toward the corner of the pen. He was shaking his head. He was shouting. "No!" he yelled. "I won't do it!" he yelled. "Cheaters!"

The hog who had been chosen the first time still couldn't find his feet. He couldn't find a single part of his body. He had chosen the pebble that meant he could go, or it had chosen him, and then it had been taken away. He charged the other hog, butted him with his head.

"You're the cheaters!" he shouted. He wheeled toward the sow. "Both of you are the cheaters."

The sow was trying hard to see around the bright light. There was the pebble, and the raised voices of the hogs, but really there was only the light: how it bathed her face.

"What?" she said.

"Both of you are the cheaters," the hog said again.

The other hog, the one with the wind blowing hard in him, heard the word and repeated it: "Cheaters!"

"I'm not a cheater," the sow said.

"Cheaters!" the hogs shouted, butting each other with their heads. Inside each of them the hunger had become a shape with jagged edges. After some time they all stopped shouting. They glared at each other.

"I won't do it," the hog with the wind in him said.

Finally the sow asked a question. She was nearly dizzy with hunger and fright, but her voice was calm — she was surprised to hear how calm. "So," she said, staring at the refusing hog, the wind-inside-him hog, "tell me the truth." She licked her lips. "No matter how many times we draw, you aren't going to stay, are you? Just so we all know where we stand."

The hog opened his mouth and the wind became the words that tumbled out. "No," he said. "I'm not building a ramp with my body, not for either of you. I'm sorry. No matter how many times we draw." He started to cry. "I'm sorry," he said, or the wind said. "I just can't."

There was some relief then, in the pen. The truth had been spoken out loud, and the situation had shifted in some small way for each of them. The refusing hog felt his head clear slightly. He lay in the corner of the pen and let the wind blow in him. I just can't, he thought.

His brother, the hog who had thought he would be free, stood in the opposite corner of the pen and looked out through the slats. He felt drained and numb. He tried to remember the days when the old man had brought food, but they seemed like a dream or a joke.

The sow wept. Night came.

"Why isn't he bringing food?" the wind-filled hog asked once.

In the morning the sow began to speak. She talked about their life, about how the man in the hut had brought food to the pen in days gone by. She described the changing seasons and how the birds flew overhead. The hogs nodded. They remembered. She told the story of the time a flock of geese had stopped in the field near the pen, and how one goose had wandered near them. She had never seen a goose up close. In the sky, geese banked on powerful wings, but on the ground, this one waddled on webbed feet. It came right to the edge of the pen and peered in, making inquisitive noises.

They all nodded, remembering the time they'd seen the goose. It had come right up to their pen and looked in at them with soft eyes. It was a sky-animal, covered in feathers. It had honked tenderly.

"The outcome's the same," the sow said after a while. "Even if there's one who *won't* stay, the outcome's the same. Do you understand?" She turned to the hog with the wind blowing in him. "You," she said. She looked him up and down. She said to the other hog, "We could build him a ramp with our bodies."

The other hog blinked. "But he didn't win when we drew."

"But he won't agree to stay, no matter how many times we draw." Inside the sow the hunger had turned from a street fight to a lullaby.

"But he's a cheater," said the hog who would have gone free. "We can't just, you know, reward that kind of behavior." He heard the words he'd used, and they confused him somehow, seemed far away. "Right?" he added.

"I don't know about that," the sow said. She shook her head as if to clear her vision. "It's more like one is better than none." She swallowed. "To survive," she said. They both took a long moment to let that sink in. The hunger inside her turned from a lullaby to an empty wooden bowl. The hog with the wind in him was out past where words could go. He was humming to himself.

"If he had been chosen, that first time, would you have built a ramp?" the sow asked.

"I don't know," said the hog who still had words. "I think so. I don't know."

"Me neither," she said. "I can't remember."

"It isn't about right and wrong," the formerly chosen hog said after a while. "Maybe it's like when you wake up and go back to sleep," he said. "Not *for* anything is what I mean, I guess. Not because you're good or anything like that."

"Yeah," the sow said. "That's how I see it, too."

"I'm pretty scared," the hog said.

The sow shook her head again and swallowed. "Yeah," she said.

They hoisted the barrel into the trough. They made a ramp with their bodies. The hog with the wind blowing in him climbed it. He clambered out of the pen.

The wind went on blowing. His brother, his sister. He looked back for a second and then started to trot. He trotted to the forest and ate. Nuts. Wild mushrooms. He ate and ate, and the hunger shrank from a chainsaw, to an insect, to a tiny dot, and disappeared, but the wind would not stop blowing, no matter how much he put in his mouth.

2. The next morning the hog awoke . . .

The next morning the hog awoke at the foot of a tree with the wind still blowing in him. Gradually his words were coming back to him, or he to them. Gradually the objects of the world were regaining a kind of solidity and coherence. It's morning, he thought. No one brought food to the pen, he thought. We drew lots to see who would be saved, he thought. His whole body started to burn.

What have I done? he thought. The sun shone brightly on the tree's rough bark.

Better stop thinking for a while, he thought, and he did stop, rooting mindlessly for nuts and wild mushrooms.

Some days passed. The hog awoke at the foot of the tree. His words had come back more clearly. It's morning, he thought. We drew lots, he thought. I called them cheaters, he thought.

The wind was blowing in him, and the wind was now the voices of the hog and the sow he had left behind.

"You," the wind said. "You left us."

The hog flinched. He swallowed.

Better stop thinking for a while, he thought.

Many days passed. The hog awoke at the foot of the tree.

"You left us," the wind said.

Better stop thinking for a while, the hog thought, but it didn't work this time. He kept thinking.

"You left us," the wind said.

The hog's body burned with shame and grief.

"You called us cheaters," the wind said.

Many days passed. The wind still blew in the hog.

"You left us," the wind said.

"I know," the hog said. His entire body was burning. "I just couldn't do it," he said. "I'm so sorry," he said.

"Sorry?" the wind said. "Where does sorry get us?"

"Not very far, I guess," the hog said.

Better stop thinking for a while, he told himself again, but again it didn't work. He kept thinking.

"You left us," the wind said.

The hog ate nuts and wild mushrooms. He slept at the foot of the tree. His whole body burned.

"I'm so sorry," he said.

"Here we go again," said the wind.

The hog awoke at the foot of the tree. He asked the wind if it would ever stop blowing.

"Do you want that?" the wind asked.

"I do," the hog said. "It would be really great."

"Yeah, well, tough shit," the wind said.

"I don't know what you want me to do," the hog said.

"There's nothing to *do*," the wind said.

"So now what?" the hog said.

"We were so hungry," the wind said.

"We were so hungry," the wind said. It blew into the hog's face.

He returned to the pen. A thick and rotten smell.

He walked around the pen in a circle, rubbed himself against the slats. It looked smaller than he remembered, just a stupid little pen next to a crumbling hut. Their bodies are in there, he thought.

"I left you," he said to the wind.

"I know," the wind said.

"There's nothing to *do*," he said to the wind.

"I know," the wind said.

"I'd like to go back to the forest and get some nuts," he told the wind, "and bring them here."

"A symbolic gesture?" the wind asked.

"I guess so, yeah. An offering."

"Well I don't know about that," the wind said. "But knock yourself out."

The hog brought nuts and wild mushrooms back from the forest to the pen. He carried them in careful mouthfuls. He made a pile outside the pen.

"This is for you," he said. "My brother, my sister." He started to cry.

"You left us," the wind said.

The hog awoke at the foot of the tree. It was a beautiful morning. He carried nuts and wild mushrooms to the pen. The smell was still there. The birds had eaten most of yesterday's offering. "I'm doing my best," he said to the wind.

The wind didn't say anything.

"I have to start somewhere," the hog said.

The wind didn't say anything.

3. The wind blew in the hog as he moved . . .

The wind blew in the hog as he moved from the forest to the
pen, from the pen to the forest, making his piles of nuts and
mushrooms. Sometimes it was a gentle wind, and he was
able to move and see and think; sometimes it was so furious
he had to stop and close his eyes, clench every muscle until
it passed. He was beginning to learn some things about the
wind—the way a log in a wood stove learns about fire. For
a long time he thought that the wind was shame, that what
blew through him was the shame of betraying his brother
and sister, but that wasn't right, not entirely. His whole body
burned sometimes with shame, with grief and hot red angry
confusion, but the wind was separate from all that. Or more
than all that. The wind was older than he had realized, first of
all, older than just his brother and sister and his own actions
that day in the pen. The wind carried all the days that had led
up to that one, all the days spent eating and talking in the pen,
their whole long lives up until that moment. And even more.
The wind carried not just their lives, but the lives of their
parents, too, and their grandparents, of all the generations
of hogs from the very beginning, all the way back, a river of

grunting eating laughing shitting fucking dreaming farting living dying hogs. Was that right? Was that what the wind was? He didn't know. It was hard to tell. When he could, when the blowing wasn't too much, he trotted back and forth with his offerings, which the birds ate.

He thought about his brother and sister. When they were barely piglets, they had been taken from their mother and brought to the pen. They had wallowed together in the same mud, the three of them. They had been rained on together, had stood together in the sunshine and the cold. Once a goose had waddled right up to their pen and peered in at them. Could any of them have known what directions their lives would take? Of course not. The wind's singing was a babble of voices, a cascade of murmuring voices.

"I'm happy to be alive," he said to the wind.

The wind didn't say anything.

"I don't know if I'm happy or not, really," he said. "It's more like I can't imagine not being alive, you know?"

The wind accelerated and turned, deepened. The wind carried the voices of his brother and sister, his parents, of all the generations of hogs — that massive, endless symphony of voices — but even that wasn't it, wasn't all of it. There was still more. Something caught in his throat. His mind spun.

The wind was all the hogs who might have been, too, the potential hogs. It was the branching of possibilities and the further branchings of each branch. Was that true? Could that be true? He breathed in and out, trying to listen.

In the wind's song he thought he heard the old age of his brother and sister, and his own death in the pen. It blew through his bones. Their lives could've gone that way — they really could've — but they hadn't, they hadn't. The wind sang the song of all the hogs who'd ever been and might have been: hogs dead early, hogs never born, hogs who failed to live up to their own deepest potentials. What sort of deepest potentials do hogs have though, really? The wind said it knew, and sang them, sang of the genius of hogs, the profound understandings possible for hogs, the complex and delicate sensations available to hogs.

"Are you serious?" the hog whispered into the roar, and the wind said it was, it was. At least, he thought that's what the wind was saying. It might have been what the wind was saying. He wasn't sure.

The wind shifted keys. The wind sang of the horrors of hogs, the vapidity and selfishness of hogs, the misery and boredom of hogs, and the possibilities radiating out from each possibility. The thwarted lives, the angry lives. The shining lives, the cramped and furious lives, the dignified and upright and terrible lives. The wind was more than the hog could bear. It sang a song too vast for him. It blew away who he was and blew right through whatever was left. "Are you serious?" the hog whispered, and the wind said that it was, it was.

The hog wrestled with the stark facts of that day in the pen. He went around and around with them in his mind. "I left you," he said to the wind, to his brother and sister in the wind. But that didn't feel true, not entirely. There was more to it than that. "It's not like I made a choice," he said, "a conscious decision or anything. It's just that I couldn't do it, couldn't make the ramp. That's all. I don't know why.

"I'm trying to understand," he said.

When he could, when the blowing wind wasn't too much, the hog trotted from the forest to the pen, piling nuts and mushrooms outside the strong boards. The wind moaned through him. He ate his food in careful mouthfuls. The strong smell around the pen had faded now. When it rained, he watched the water run down the pen's strong slats; when the sun shone, he watched the heat bake the thick posts. The wind carved a path through his body.

"I just want to sort it all out," he said to the wind. "I really do."

He carried food from the forest and piled it outside the pen where the birds ate it. His breathing swirled in and out of him.

"I wonder sometimes if you're fate," he said to the wind.

"Fate?" the wind asked.

"Yeah," the hog said. "You know, like destiny or something?"

"Not even close," the wind said.

He carried food from the forest to the pen.

"Well, then," he said, "maybe time?"

"I beg your pardon?" said the wind.

"Time," he said. "Like what you are is the passage of time, days going by. Blowing me forward, blowing me through my life."

"Not even close to close," said the wind.

His breathing moved in and out of his body.

"We've been through a lot together," he told the wind. He trotted back and forth to the pen and made piles of food for the birds.

"Sure," said the wind. "If you say so."

4. That's how the days and weeks passed . . .

That's how the days and weeks passed. Months passed. Years. Until the summer morning that the wooden slats of the pen rotted all the way through, and the hog tore it apart. He knocked the boards down methodically. They gave easily. The trough was there; the rain barrel was there. Two twisted objects he could not look at were there, on the ground. He butted and stomped and broke the wood into pieces, panting, until only splinters remained. He stood amid the wreckage for a long time, waiting for his breathing to return to normal. He was aware of the sky stretching above him, and of a slight pain in his hooves from the stomping. He still had not looked closely at the twisted objects. For the first time in years, the wind stopped blowing, just for a few moments.

Then it started again.

After that, the hog didn't visit the site of the pen very often. He spent his days and nights in the forest. The sun rose and set; the moon rose and set. "I did what I did," he said to the wind. "I don't know why. And now I'm living on into the next day. Do you see what I mean?"

The wind didn't say anything, but the hog didn't mind. What he felt now for the wind was a kind of familiarity. It served as a compass point for him, a way of orienting himself in the world. When he inhaled, he breathed in the wind, and when he exhaled, he breathed out the wind. Each breath was a small wind in the vast wind that surrounded him, although sometimes even that wasn't true and each breath was the whole of the vast wind itself. He moved more slowly these days; his body often hurt.

"Are you sure you aren't time?" he asked the wind again.

"I'm not time," the wind laughed, swirling in and out of his face. "You aren't even in the ballpark."

"Oh," said the hog, though he didn't understand. He breathed in and out.

"Not even next to the ballpark," the wind said.

The hog lay underneath the tree. He was very old. Down his left side there was a kind of pain that was different from the usual aching. A new pain.

"Well, whatever you are," he said.

"Yes?" said the wind.

"I'm pretty grateful to you," he said. "Staying with me all these years." He thought about his brother and his sister, that day in the pen. He had been so young then. He had left them behind to starve. He remembered the mornings when the old man had brought them food, how the trough had nearly overflowed with food.

"Grateful?" asked the wind.

The pain in his side was blossoming, spreading into his limbs. He was dying.

"Yeah," he said. He took a long breath.

He remembered the day a goose had come down from the sky, how it had laid its soft eyes on him.

"Grateful?" asked the wind gently.

"Yeah," he said. He meant it. He mostly meant it. The sun was shining through the branches of the tree, the slowly waving branches. He understood that his life was almost over. Just a few more minutes.

He remembered his mother. Lying against her warm, thick side, together with his siblings. He could feel their bodies against him, the skin smell, the sweet taste of milk. He didn't know if he felt grateful or not, actually. Maybe he didn't. It was hard to say, so hard to sum it all up, to keep it from turning into something else.

The sunlight through the branches.

The pain was sharper now.

They drank her milk until they fell asleep.

LESSON

Boy on a stone wall, dark eyes, curly-headed, maybe four years old. His father stood in front of him with his arms open. I remember this. It was spring, in a small town in the province of Buenos Aires. Saltá, mijo, the father whispered, Jump. And the boy was scared, but the father said it again, Jump, I'll catch you, and the boy did and the father stepped back. I remember the father stepping back.

The boy landed on his knees in the gravel. A crunching sound.

That's so you'll learn never to trust anyone, the father said, and lifted the boy to his chest.

I was passing by, I saw the whole thing. Staring at the culvert's thick green grass, lost in my adolescent burning and spiraling, and a man was teaching his son about the world, right there in front of my face.

Were there crows above us? I seem to remember crows, their caws scraping the sky, but I could be wrong, or mixing memories from separate occasions. It doesn't matter.

Today, in a game she invented, my daughter, almost six, asked me to close my eyes while she led me by the hand through the playground near our apartment in Oakland. My daughter's hand was small in mine. Her hair uncombed and wild.

I closed my eyes tight. I took a careful step forward into the dark, then another one. I let her guide me. I wanted to open my eyes, but I didn't. I didn't cheat. It was dizzying, like falling through space. I took another step, then another, my feet crunching the gravel.

"Keep them closed," she ordered, and I did. All around us, crows called out.

THE EXACT THING

We had nowhere to go. It was January. Lucy was driving me around. Her car's heat had busted and the white clouds of our breath fogged the windshield. We had to keep rolling the windows down.

"Did you ever think that chattering teeth are like rows of birds crashing into the ground?" I asked, and she ignored me. We were pretty high.

The airplane materialized right there above us: the lights along its wings and body, the individual lit-up windows. It was freshly washed and painted, dropping fast. It was tilted at a strange angle. We pulled over to the curb.

"We need to pray for them," Lucy said, lacing her fingers together. She didn't look at me.

The plane kept sinking until it went out of sight, and I waited for the sky to explode, sirens and flames, the moaning of emergency vehicles.

"Here it comes," I shouted, pumping my fist. "Here it comes, yeah!"

Lucy whispered under her breath.

Nothing happened.

"Yeah," I said again.

A minute later, I realized that we were over by the airport. But we didn't know that then, so it counts. The exact thing we did counts.

TREE, BIRD, SPOON

In the desert outside of everything, there is one tree, one bird, there is one iron spoon. Sometimes the bird and the spoon get inside the tree. Sometimes the tree and the bird get inside the spoon. Sometimes the spoon and the tree get inside the bird. This is how they spend their time: the freezing nights, the mornings, the endless hot bright afternoons.

THE SQUIRRELS

She can no longer locate her words; they aren't where she left them. She hesitates, she points, she makes a sound.

"The squirrels," she begins, then stops. She looks around the room. She doesn't mean squirrels.

"My firepan is growing," she says by way of explanation.

Her husband is pale, furious, making arrangements. The tumors in her brain are getting larger. He opens and closes his hands.

Her eyes are unnaturally clear, luminous almost. "See those eyes?" the nurse says to the social worker on the steps outside and the social worker sighs, nods, licks her lips. The overheated room smells like urine and orchids, the flowers in large arrangements on the dresser, on the windowsill, on the floor.

The nurse and the social worker go down the steps to the sidewalk, chat about other things for a bit before heading for their cars.

"Holly is coming tomorrow," the husband says, touching her shoulder.

"Our feather," she says.

"Our hollow," she says after a while.

He sits on the edge of the bed, stands again.

Her hand, her right hand, is contracted so severely that she shouts with pain when it's touched. The nails were left untrimmed for many weeks and they grew into the palm, cut through, and the wounds in the palm infected. "I didn't know," the husband tells the daughter on the phone, his voice choking, and the daughter weeps because of her mother's illness and her father's bewilderment and her own crashing sense of the merciless world. She packs blindly, not folding the clothes.

"I want," the mother says. She brings her head forward off the pillow. "Where's that tower?"

Some days are better than others, though. "I'm calmer than I thought I'd be," she'd said once, just a few mornings ago.

Holly arrives, red-eyed. She wraps her arms around her trembling father. "I'm here now, Dad," she tells him. She is aware of how frail he is, of the tension in his thin frame.

The three of them are together on the bed. The nurse with the gentle voice stops by to say good night. She presses the husband's hand, takes a long look at the daughter. "Is there anything else I can get you?" she asks and the daughter shakes her head. "We're just fine," she says brightly, and blushes, her cheeks filling with blood. The nurse starts to say something else, stops. The daughter swallows. She says, "We're just fine" again. Her face is burning. The father opens and closes his hands. The door shuts with a click.

The lights are dimmer now, only a lamp on the dresser. Painted flowers on the lampshade, real flowers all around. The bulb shines steadily, without flickering. "The door was licky orange," the mother mumbles once. "The grass."

They give her ice chips, sit next to the bed. Her breathing is still strong.

"I didn't walk that far," she says.

No more traffic outside. The three of them are together.

"Put my hat away."

MEMORIAL

A stack of AA chips carefully placed on the newspaper vending machine outside the liquor store. *To thine own self be true, God grant me the serenity.*

A neat stack: red on yellow on blue.

One month. Two months. Six.

THOMAS JEFFERSON

They're hitting the kid on the ground with a bottle. Group standing around. Richard's watching—ten years old, the youngest. The bottle is label-peeling Miller Lite brown glass. The kid on the ground wears a blue sweatshirt, jeans. His straight blond hair covers part of his face.

The kid hitting him is big, even bigger in his bulky jacket. He's rapping the bottle against the ground-kid, rap against skull, rap into ribs, hard. "Don't move," he says. "You move and I'll break this on you." He's holding back. Slap of glass on bone. Red marks on ground-kid's face, they'll bruise. "Don't want this to break, do you? Get cut if it breaks." The crowd is watching, Richard is watching.

Later, Richard will wonder about the thought. It comes with all the authority of a dream, just that clear. In the thought, Richard rescues the kid on the ground. The kid becomes an antelope Richard saw on television once, a baby, velvet-nubbed horns, skinny forelegs. Richard will adopt this antelope. He will name the antelope Thomas Jefferson.

Tommy's wet trembling eyes. Tommy's tongue on Richard's palm. The tongue is dry, rough—like a cat's—when Richard brings him grass to eat, grass from the park by his house.

TWO

VOICES OF SMOKE

Molly worked with Trisha waiting tables. Richard used to see her when he went to pick Trisha up. He'd drive Trisha home to their apartment where the pigeons cooed and gurgled on the fire escape, and he'd think about Molly's tongue, the shape of her thighs.

"How was work?" he'd ask Trisha, and she'd shrug.

She hardly spoke to him those last months they were together, just mumbled about groceries and bills. Even before the night he pushed her into the kitchen table, she'd been withdrawn—but after that she acted as if speaking exhausted her, as if it wasted energy she needed for some immense, delicate task.

Chicago summer. In the evenings, Richard would take a beer onto the fire escape, dangle his feet over the traffic three stories below. He'd fill his mouth, swallow; the pigeons would strut and flurry over the black metal rods. From the bar on the corner, thuds of music floated to him, along with voice-scraps, engine noise. Every few minutes the L went by two blocks away, rattling and clanging, shooting off sparks. Often, at night, if he saw the train pass out of the corner of his eye, he'd mistake the sparking of the wheels on the metal tracks for the flashing lights of a police car or ambulance. He'd jerk his head, flinch before he realized.

Inside, Trisha would sit at the kitchen table and eat, slowly, painstakingly. She'd let food dissolve on her tongue with her eyes closed. Richard couldn't stand to watch her do it. She'd eat a bowl of salt, a few grains at a time; or a candy bar, shaving curls of chocolate off with a knife. She'd eat a loaf of French bread, a grapefruit, a fried egg. She'd escape into herself, into the flavors, while Richard got drunk and watched the cars go by underneath him.

There was something he couldn't help about going to see Molly, even when he'd promised himself he wouldn't. It was like working his finger underneath a scab, like turning down the Bacas' street, back in high school, and knowing he would knock on their door, even if later he would wish he hadn't.

This was in a town called Butler, in West Texas. That's where they lived then. Semis on the highway, dust blowing in spirals, no sidewalks on most of the streets. The Bacas were friends of his father's.

Their eyes made him talk louder, his voice brassy and vulgar. When he was at their house, Richard ate more, sprawled his body across the furniture, flexed the muscles in his arms and chest. He chewed with his mouth open, laughed a lot. They hung onto his every word, their faces grief-stricken and stunned. They leaned against each other, watching him.

He felt powerful after being with the Bacas, felt strong, young. But if his dad asked why he was home late, where he'd been, Richard would feel a surge of almost-shame. He'd want to lie. His dad's eyes were close-set, green, staring from between his thin beard and eyebrows. "I worked late," Richard would say. "I was just talking to some people."

On the fire escape, Richard thought about Molly's voice, Molly's body, Molly's hands. The way she said his name, like she'd been thinking it all day. When he was with her, he had a mindless, physical purpose. Their bodies driving against each other. Tongues and teeth and fingernails. The small satisfaction of calmly wrecking his life. He stayed out on the fire escape, traffic swirling beneath him, until the lights in the building across the street had blinked out, one by one. Every single window dark.

He moved inside. Trisha was at the kitchen table, melting flavors in her mouth, not speaking. She was barefoot, in jeans and a worn orange T-shirt. Richard opened the refrigerator and twisted the top off a bottle of beer, stared aimlessly at the containers of food, the old take-out boxes and wilting vegetables.

"Hey, Trish. You want some peanut butter?" He pulled out a jar. "This would be good, wouldn't it? You could get a toothpick, maybe?"

Her eyes were closed. On the table stood an empty ceramic bowl and a container of Kool-Aid. She was holding a glass with a few inches of purple liquid in it up to her mouth, straining it through her teeth a tiny bit at a time, concentrating, rapt. Lost in herself. Doing it just to provoke him, to render him unnecessary.

"Come on, honey." He moved toward her. "You don't want a nice toothpickful of peanut butter? It's creamy."

She opened her eyes, glared at him, and ran her tongue over her dark-stained teeth. Cleaning them. "I don't want any."

He shrugged. "No peanut butter, then. If you say so." From a shelf in the door he pulled a plastic bottle of salad dressing and shook it in his fist.

"Hey, Trish? How about some of this? I could get you a straw." She said nothing, and he laughed once at her, a short joyless bark, before setting the bottle on the counter and going into the bedroom. The refrigerator door swung slowly closed. On his way out of the kitchen he turned out the light with a rough swipe at the wall. He paused for her reaction, but she just stayed hunched over in the darkness, tasting.

A lot of nights she'd fall asleep there, in one of the kitchen's stiff chairs, and he'd tiptoe by her in the morning. When Trisha was asleep, her face was calmer, more relaxed. Her head rested on the table. Richard liked to watch her sleeping, her hair spread wild over the plates. The thin skin of her eyelids. It made him feel tender toward her, like she was a child. He'd eat breakfast quietly, watching her in the early morning light, and he'd slip down the stairs where the tenderness would fade almost immediately in the day's stomach-gnawing, in his constant, punishing dissatisfaction.

It was his first year as a substitute teacher. Every morning he had to get up early, put on a shirt with buttons and tuck it in, call for the assignment. He'd crawl into his rattling car through the passenger door since it was the only one that opened. He'd make his way across the seat, avoiding the gearshift, bringing his knees awkwardly up to his chest and under the steering wheel, and he'd drive the brutal traffic to work. When he arrived in some new, unfamiliar parking lot, he'd do the same thing in reverse, wiggling across the seat and out the passenger door into another day, watched idly by whoever happened to be standing around.

The schools were strange in the summer, hallways almost empty, and his footsteps echoed off the rows of lockers, the peeling walls. In the classrooms, the students were always restless, aware of hot, clear days outside. His face felt stiff and wooden as he called their names for roll or went over the assignments or sat uncomfortably in someone else's chair waiting for a bell to ring.

He worked all over the city. The kids were alien to him. They dismissed him immediately when he entered a room, made him feel skinny and white-bread as their eyes licked his body, made him feel awkward in his clothes. All that black skin, brown skin.

Even the white kids, though—they weren't like him, weren't like he had been at their age. They were urban, looser with their shoulders and arms. Their clothes hung off them, only suggested the bone and muscle beneath. They seemed to him to be always jostling and shoving each other in the hallways, always throwing each other into lockers for a joke. They talked in code. He never knew what their lives were like. At most schools, when he left in the afternoon, he'd walk through a group of young men in front of the door. Conversation would break off as he passed. Eyes would flick over him—up then down.

He'd yell at the kids sometimes, when they wouldn't be quiet, when they wouldn't listen. "Shut the fuck up," he screamed once at a roomful of sophomores. There was silence. Faces went blank or angry. Most students looked at their feet, stunned, or at the wall behind him, expressions careful and closed down. A few, the guys in back, tilted their heads, chins forward and to the side, eyeing him.

That was a mistake, he thought, but it was too late to undo it, so he threw his hands in the air and repeated himself, quieter this time. "Just all of you shut the fuck up."

Walls with water stains. Crushing boredom, the crash of voices, fear of violence. One morning, in the main office of a high school on the West Side, a group of teachers talked about a dog someone had found in a field behind the gym. A student had beaten it to death with a milk crate. One woman, short, middle-aged, hair to the middle of her back, covered her mouth with her hand. "I don't know how much more of this I can take," she said, and everyone murmured in agreement.

That afternoon, he walked out behind the school to see the dog's body. Birds darted through the grass, exploding up in a flutter of wings when Richard got too close. The dog was smaller than he expected, bloody fur, broken ribs sticking out. The crate lay nearby, clotted blood on the orange plastic. There were patches of blood on the ground, too, dark, almost black, and flies walking over the dog's face and sides.

Richard crouched and stared. The afternoon was hot and still, but no smell yet. He pulled up a weed and stripped it, staining the tips of his fingernails green. Dog blood on the ground, dog skin going leather-stiff in the sun. For a wild moment, he considered urinating on the body, and half-stood, reaching for his zipper, before he caught himself. He glanced over his shoulder at the school, three stories of classroom windows pointed at him. All those eyes. The idea felt right, though—pissing on the beaten body—and he imagined a warm stream disturbing the flies, falling in drops from the fur, turning the bloodstains on the ground to mud.

He hadn't meant to push Trisha into the table that night. The whole way to the hospital, drunk, trying to stay in his lane, trying not to panic at the sight of her bleeding, he yelled over and over, "I didn't mean to do that. You know I didn't mean to do that." Lights from other cars, from signs, swam in blurs across the windshield. He sobered up in the waiting room, slumped in a molded plastic chair, staring at the patterned carpet while they put in her stitches. A television bolted to the wall yammered about nothing. She had cut her head and bruised her back and face.

He hadn't meant to do it. Really he hadn't. That afternoon he hadn't gone straight home after work. He was restless, drove around in the heat, sweat sticky on his back. He drove north, into the suburbs. In Evanston, near the university, a car full of women passed him with their shirts off, leaning out the window, cheering.

He accelerated to catch up, and one of the women leaned out the back window, raised her arms over her head, laughed. Her mouth was wide open, her arms above her head, her half-naked body leaning out the window. The pale curve of her. They were all laughing and Richard, staring, reached to roll down his window, to say something, his throat constricted, but the handle came off in his hand, like always, and he threw it against the floor. The window wouldn't roll down. He was suddenly claustrophobic, suffocating, trapped in the car—hot metal box, no escape—and outside those women, college girls, gliding by in the afternoon, skin smooth, and sunshine on it. He started drinking as soon as he got home.

That was in the spring. Afterwards, he didn't think about that night very often, but on the day he saw the dog's dead beaten body behind the school, it came back to him. He remembered Trisha on the kitchen floor after the table collapsed. He hadn't even pushed her that hard, really. She was clicking her teeth together and grimacing. Her hands were raised to her head.

The image was still with him as he drove to pick her up from work. "Some kid killed a dog behind the school today," he told her when she got into the car. Her face was tired and drawn, pale. He glanced in the restaurant window as he pulled out of the lot, but didn't see Molly, only customers seated at the long wooden tables, their faces lit by the fake gas lamps hanging on the walls. Trisha stared at the dashboard. "What do you mean?"

"What do you think I mean? Some kid found a stray dog and killed it." He drummed his fingers on the steering wheel. "With a milk crate. Unbelievable, isn't it?"

He pulled out of the parking lot. For a few blocks, they didn't talk. "How do you know?" Trisha asked him.

"About the dog?"

She nodded.

"All the teachers were talking about it. The kid did it last night, I guess, and someone saw him. They were trying to figure out whether to call the cops or what."

"Did you see it?" Her face was turned toward him. He slowed at a stop sign, then raced through without completely stopping.

"No," he said, checking the rearview mirror, surprised at his lie. "Why? Do you want to go see it? I know where it is."

She made a disgusted sound and shook her head. She didn't ask about it again until later. He was in the kitchen, light reflecting from clean surfaces of table, counter, refrigerator, watching the small television set, and she came in and sat across from him.

"What happened to the dog?"

"Beat to death." She looked down. "I told you," he said. "With a milk crate. Can you imagine?"

"Stop it."

The television laugh track went off, applause and hooting. Trisha pulled a paper napkin from a stack and smoothed it on the table's surface. Richard tried to grin, but his cheeks resisted, stretched uncomfortably.

"What kind of dog was it?" With her fingernails, she tore the napkin into strips.

"I don't know."

She looked up, head tilted to the side. Her voice was accusing. "Is it still there?"

He hesitated. She leaned forward suddenly and clicked off the remote. "Is it?"

"Probably." He shrugged and slumped away from her in his seat. "Janitors aren't going to want to deal with something like that."

"We need to go bury it," she said. When he started to laugh, she stood, balling the shredded napkin up in her hand and dropping it onto the tabletop. "I'm not kidding," she said. "Come on."

He hesitated for a moment, looking at her. He did what she told him. He lifted the car keys from their hook by the door and when she came out of the bathroom with a thick towel, he locked up and followed her down the stairs. Outside their apartment, she waited for him to crawl in the passenger door and over to the driver's side before she got in. "We need to buy a shovel," she said. "Go to that big hardware store by my work."

Trisha paid for the shovel with her credit card. They drove toward the school. Richard had never been through these neighborhoods after dark. He watched the cars next to him at red lights, angling his eyes over their hoods, not looking directly at their drivers.

Entire blocks seemed abandoned to him, lunar, no one on the sidewalk or on the front steps of the apartments. Windows boarded up. Rubble. A little later, though, in front of a liquor store with grates over the windows, there were suddenly people everywhere, spilling off the sidewalk into the street. Groups of men stood talking, or sat on milk crates watching the traffic.

Richard let a long breath out through his teeth when they were past. "Do we have to do this now?"

"Yes." Trisha sat in the passenger seat with her knees drawn up, tangled in the seat belt. Her voice was flat. When they got to the school, he parked under a streetlight and climbed out the passenger door after her. Clouds of bugs, circling the light, cast huge flitting shadows all around them. In the dark field, crickets shrieked.

At first Richard was glad to see no people around. Then he imagined a figure crouching in the weeds, waiting for them. "We should've brought a flashlight," he complained, picking his way through the grass, carrying the shovel. Trisha, walking behind him, said nothing. The bass from a car radio grew out of the darkness, a deep thump that faded slowly after the car passed. They stumbled and searched in the weeds for a few minutes. Finally, his eyes adjusted to the night, Richard saw the dog's still shape on the ground. It was beginning to smell of rot, sweet and dense, a stink he tried not to breathe.

Trisha squatted, lifted the dead animal to wrap it in the towel. She lowered it back down. She stroked its head and chest softly. Disgusted, Richard turned away from the sight of her hands on the body. He tore up plants by the roots until he'd cleared an area big enough for a grave. He pushed the shovel into the ground with his weight. Trisha sat on the ground, her hand on the body. She was crying.

"Trish." He stopped digging, surprised, and bent over, his hand on her back. "What is it?" She shook her head without looking up, pushed away at his arm.

He started digging again, stomping the shovel down, lifting. She never makes sense anymore, he thought, beginning to sweat. She sits for hours licking cloves of garlic, or eating graham cracker crumbs out of a bowl. She doesn't even know about Molly, he told himself, and he was furious at her.

The night overflowed with the sounds of crickets, and of cars passing, their engines coughing or roaring, sometimes music from their radios splashing out, sometimes voices. All the sounds of a living night, in summer, in a city, mixing with the whimpers Trisha made.

Tears and mucus marked her face. He wished she would stop. He checked behind him to make sure no one was there. His shovel rose and fell. Beneath the thick, dry crust, the soft ground came up easily. When he was done digging, Trisha placed the dog into the trench, weeping harder and harder, her hands running over its legs and paws, its snout, its ears.

When she saw the milk crate, she got to her feet and stood over it. "Richard?"

"Yeah." The crate was on its side. He wished he'd thought to kick it away, into the weeds where she wouldn't have found it.

"How?" she asked.

He cleared his throat. "I don't really know, Trish."

She cried harder than he'd ever seen her cry before. She said his name one more time, "Richard," unbelieving, and he stepped toward her with his arms out and she raised her hands in front of her, keeping him back. "Don't touch me!"

Richard stopped as if she'd slapped him. He looked over his shoulder to see who had heard, but there was no one.

When he was very young, Richard had lived with his dad in an apartment complex outside of Jackson, Mississippi. He remembers the slosh of blue water in a swimming pool, in the sun, and the tangled fibers of a carpet, and cars driving slowly through a parking lot like sharks. At least he thinks that was Jackson. He and his dad moved around a lot. Most of his early memories aren't tied to a place. Sometimes he stares at an intersection, or a fat moon over a series of warehouses, and knows it reminds him of somewhere he's seen before, but he doesn't know where.

Richard's dad was a brooding, impractical man. He liked to read, liked to drink. Before Richard was born he had worked for the union, but the years of Richard's childhood he worked anywhere—factories or offices or stores. He sold shoes, operated a bulldozer, moved furniture. He filled out tax forms, painted, welded.

"Why here?" he'd say, looking around impatiently, when his job chafed at him, or his life. "Why not somewhere else?"

They lived all over the West and South, moving once a year or more. One summer, Richard lived with his mom and her new boyfriend in Montana. His parents had never gotten divorced officially, custody was something they decided as they went along. Richard never knew whose decision it was, but one afternoon that fall his dad's pickup was in the driveway, come to take him back, and he never lived with his mom again.

When Richard was about to start high school, his dad decided they should stay in one place until graduation. He got a job in Butler, working for a company that sold farm equipment, and they lived there four years, just as he'd promised.

Butler. Railroad tracks behind their small house, the sun like a hammer on the flat, dusty land. Those were the years Richard would go to see his father's friends the Bacas. Their son Tony had taken his own life the winter before Richard met them. Richard had never known Tony, never knew why he had walked out to the garage with a shotgun, but he knew that when he went over to the Bacas' house, he was important. They needed him.

Their house was stale inside, smelled like cigarettes. When Richard knocked on the door, Mr. Baca got up stiffly from the couch to shake his hand and slap him on the back. They sat in the kitchen and Mrs. Baca served him chocolate ice cream in a plastic bowl, the television murmuring from the other room. "How's school?" she asked. Her face was thin, faint traces of hair on her upper lip. "How's your dad?" "How are you?"

They leaned in close to hear. Sometimes he offered to do the dishes or mow the lawn, but they'd thank him and refuse. "You're a good kid," Mr. Baca would say, and slap him on the back again, thick-handed. Richard walked to their door, past the dining room table covered with stacks of old hunting magazines. Outside, the tall lights hummed on their poles, made bright circles on the street. Walking from their house, Richard felt unbelievably strong and alive. He'd pick up a stick and swat rocks with it, leaning back and launching them into the night.

Years later, Richard visited Texas again, with Trisha, not long after they met. They took a bus from Sacramento across the desert to Big Bend, on the Mexican border, and camped there for a week.

"I used to live in a place like this," he told her on the bus. "When I was a kid." They had just bumped over a series of railroad tracks on the outskirts of a small, dusty town. "Probably one of the most boring places on earth," Richard said, and she asked how old he was then and he said high school and the conversation slid on, a laughing, sparkling thing that lasted all through that camping trip, and beyond.

Trisha with a backpack and a big silly sun-hat. Trisha's face visible under the bright desert moon. It was hot and dusty and windy, and they didn't have enough water, and they were worried about rattlesnakes, and they both sunburned—but they were allied against the discomfort. They shared water, rubbed lotion on each other's peeling skin, laughed for hours imagining the inevitable snake attack.

They were in it together, and on the long bus ride back across New Mexico and Arizona to the West Coast they were tender with each other. "Look," Trisha said, and pointed out clouds. The bus rolled through long valleys of red dirt, past scrubby pines and junipers, bluffs with sheer walls.

Every few miles, it seemed, they saw rusty schoolbuses, sitting in the middle of nowhere, in the sun. "Here's where they grow schoolbuses," Richard explained, nodding wisely.

"Some of these look too ripe," she said.

"Yeah, you got to pick them at the right time."

That night they slept uncomfortably, tangled around each other on the bus seats. Every time Richard woke up, he stroked Trisha's wrist, or kissed her forehead, or mumbled her name. Back in Sacramento, before the glow of their trip had faded, they decided to move somewhere together. Talking over an unfolded map of the United States, laughing and intentionally mispronouncing city names, they chose Chicago almost at random.

There must have been reasons, reasons that seemed good at the time. Very soon, Richard couldn't remember what those reasons had been. But there they were, there they found themselves, in a vacant lot at night, almost a year later.

"Come on, Trish," Richard said. "Let's finish this and go home." She had stopped crying, but was still crouched over the dog's body in the shallow trench. She didn't move. "Trisha, I'm going to bury this, okay? So we can go home?" He picked up a shovelful of dirt.

"No," she said, and her voice was flat. "I'm going to do it." She took the shovel from his hands. She filled the grave methodically, scooping the loose dirt from the pile he had made and letting it drop with a soft thump.

Chicago was a mistake. They shouldn't have done it. The apartment Richard and Trisha rented was too small, only a bedroom, kitchen, and bathroom. They could go nowhere in it without hearing the other person move or rustle or cough. Their bills were more than they expected, especially heat through the long, first winter.

In March, one night, at a party for the people Trisha worked with, Richard met Molly. He pretended to think her name was Polly, which made her laugh. After a few minutes, she started calling him Pichard.

A week later, in Molly's apartment for the first time, Richard felt like he was standing outside his body watching himself act. He was kissing her. His hand was inside her shirt, on her stomach. His fingers were tracing the soft skin of her thigh. If he were sober, he thought, he wouldn't be doing this, but he wasn't sober, and he was doing this, and he got home very late, after Trisha had gone to sleep.

It stayed with him, that feeling of watching himself from the outside, all through the spring and summer, as he and Trisha slid away from each other, now with a momentum they couldn't control. They spoke less, hardly ever touched, hardly ever kissed. He shoved her hard into the kitchen table one night, watched arms and legs and plates crash to the floor.

She started surrounding herself with small piles of food, tasting, tasting with her eyes closed, while he sat on the fire escape with the gurgling pigeons and watched the cars go by. One night they drove across the city to bury a dog, and three weeks later, after another day full of helpless, silent hostility, she started packing. Richard watched her get her stuff together, and she moved out the next morning.

After that, he almost never heard from her. Which didn't surprise him. But he lost track of Molly, too, which did in a way. He hadn't expected that. He thought about her sometimes, of course, but he could never quite summon up the energy to call her or stop by. He just didn't want to. The timing was never right. The idea wore him out.

Richard's new apartment was small, but at least he was the only one in it. He went to work and came home. He left his clothes on the floor, let dishes pile up in the sink. On weekends, he didn't shave. He bought himself some plants to take care of, watering them carefully, moving the pots from window to window.

One morning, late in the fall, he worked again at the school on the West Side where he and Trisha had buried the dog. It wasn't a place he liked to go. Once he'd taken the day off entirely to avoid it. The classrooms were big, full of light, bright blue paint peeling off the walls. He was subbing for a science teacher who'd left him a movie and a mimeographed sheet of questions for the students to answer.

Richard wheeled the TV/VCR to the front of his first class and lowered the shades. A student turned out the light and pushed play and the movie began. The movie was about the sun. Richard didn't follow it very closely. Around him, the students rustled and murmured and breathed.

Tongues of fire licked into space from the sun's surface. Computer-generated images rotated around each other, representing the planets' formal dance through the solar system. From the back of the room, Richard watched the flickering television. His students had their heads down on their desks, or were whispering to each other, fidgeting in their seats, but he ignored them. Outside, in the field behind the school, the dog's body must have rotted away under the ground, skin and muscle dissolving into the moist dirt. Maybe some strips of fur left like banners on the bones.

The sun is a million times larger than the Earth. The temperature at its core is twenty-five million degrees Fahrenheit. The announcer's voice was slow and deep, citing figures and statistics, posing questions and immediately answering them. He used terms like "breathtaking" and "sheer immensity." Music swelled and crashed. And then the movie was over and the screen went blue. Richard handed out the question sheet and told the students to work on it quietly until the bell rang. He opened the shades.

After showing the movie to his last class of the morning, he didn't pass the question sheet out right away. He stood in front of the room and looked at the kids' faces, their hair and hands, the way the light reflected off their skin. He thought for the first time how strangely, incredibly young they all were. They had so many decades ahead of them.

"My name's Richard," he said, then stopped to swallow and clear his throat. "I've been a sub for about a year." The kids looked at him blankly. Someone laughed.

"What did you think of that movie?" he asked, and there was silence.

"It sucked," someone hissed from the back of the room, and the kids all grinned. Richard grinned, too. He sat on the ledge by the window to feel the cool air.

Toward the end of class, he stood up. He was restless, as if a sudden gust of wind could lift and carry him. "Who thinks I can touch the ceiling?" he asked, and a kid in front said, "No chance."

He leaped up a couple of times, taking a running start and bending way down before he jumped, but he couldn't reach, not even close. The ceiling must have been fifteen feet high. The kids were all laughing at him. "Oh, well," he said, unable to keep from grinning again. "Worth a shot."

The no-chance kid punched another kid in the shoulder, over and over, cracking up.

Richard went outside during lunch, sat on the hood of his car in his coat and ate the French fries he had bought in the cafeteria. They were greasy and limp, but he even licked his finger to get the crumbs from the bottom of the cardboard container. The grasses in the field behind the school moved like water in the wind.

When he had pushed her into the kitchen table that night, Trisha had curled herself on the floor with her arms shielding her head and her small face twisted in fear. He had stood over her, snarling. Normally, Trisha was beautiful, in her fragile, distracted way, but she wasn't beautiful then.

He had reduced her.

In the afternoon he watched the images of the movie repeat themselves—swirls of fire, solar wind, a cartoon stick figure walking through space to demonstrate distances. He was getting tired, wished he'd had a cup of coffee with lunch. His last two classes dripped by slowly, the clock hands almost motionless.

The final bell, when it came, was a release. The kids rushed into the noise of the hallway, leaving Richard to sit in the empty classroom until their shouts and echoes faded. He gathered his things and locked the door, picked his way down the stairs to the main office. He left the room key with the secretary. In the parking lot, he climbed in his car's passenger side and took off his coat. The sky was high and clear and blue, the tang and ache of autumn in the air. He sat behind the wheel for a moment without turning the ignition. He didn't want to go home.

He started the engine, finally, and drove under the impossible arch of sky. He was very tired. He wondered what it must be like to beat a dog to death in a field. The milk crate rising and falling, the animal rolling and whimpering in the dirt. Before the shame hit, and the self-revulsion, would you lose yourself in the violence? Would you forget your life, forget who you were?

Angels sing at moments like that. Voices of smoke, voices of silver.

Then you have to run away through the dark streets with blood on your clothes.

THE EMPEROR'S SWANS

The swans are beautiful; they are so lovely. They move on the water like part of the water, or part of the sky. They are a distillation of something else, a vagueness made precise, floating on the surface of the emperor's lake.

In his old age, in his senility, the emperor is becoming still more austere. Always he's been a cruel man, but now the thought of his impending death makes him colder, more frantic. He paces along the shore, watching the swans. The swans are his. He prizes them. His attendants keep their eyes carefully on the ground.

The emperor's six sons scheme and jockey for power. They move in a shifting web of alliances. Each of them, fearing poison, eats separately, hunched over his plate.

One night, the youngest—just a boy—dreams of roasting the emperor's swans until their hot grease splatters the coals. In the dream, he eats the entire flock with his bare hands. He rips the bloody meat with his teeth. He chews up the swans' eyes and brains, their entrails. He licks the marrow from the broken bird-bones while his father and his older brothers watch helplessly.

It's just a dream. In the morning he wakes to sunlight, unrelenting tension, the soft footsteps of his fat valet. With his eyes, he traces the familiar pattern of alternating dark and light wood in the beams of his ceiling.

The next night, he dreams again. This time he tears pieces of tender meat from the swans' bodies and feeds them to his brothers. His brothers eat from his hand like horses— rough, warm lips—and he strokes their sides. With a stiff brush, he combs his brothers' manes. They gallop together in a field.

In the morning, awake, he looks at the ceiling.

Almost by the hour, the emperor's health declines. The haggard sons plot in whispers with their advisors. Days pass. An anonymous note warns the youngest son not to sleep in his own bed anymore. One of his brothers, on two separate occasions, counsels him to avoid a certain servant, but gives no details. The youngest nods.

That night, he sleeps in an alcove behind the basement kitchens and dreams that he has become one of the swans. His neck is powerful and long. He bends it this way and that, looking up at the sky, down at the ripples he makes as he swims with the others.

After a while, he leaves the group behind. He glides to the shore. Shaking drops of water from his feathers, he rises from the shallows and waddles across the gardens to the barbecue pit. Everyone is there: his father, older brothers, crowds of servants. They are all watching.

He hoists himself onto the coals.

THE EMPEROR'S KITCHEN

I'm the baker's assistant, but I got plans.
  And the baker's getting old.

A METHOD FOR APPEASING JACKALS

Make a jackal from the pieces of jackal in your own body and offer the jackal you have made to the jackals that surround you. Sing the appropriate song: *Jackals, I give you a jackal / made from my own body / jackals, a delicate feast!*

The jackal you make from the jackal-pieces of your own body must be a living jackal. The jackals that surround you will eat a dead jackal of course (they're scavengers)—but after eating they will not be appeased, which means that you must locate only the living pieces of jackal within your own body.

Most of the preparation for this method of appeasing jackals, in fact, involves patiently locating and gathering together the living jackal pieces of your own body, and usually after gathering the pieces, you no longer wish to employ the method. Usually you wish instead to be appeased yourself—who can blame you really, after all that work?— and you abandon the non-jackal pieces of your own body, living or not, let them drop off like a man who hates his job drops his too-tight slacks after a long day.

You can stretch then, finally, stretch your living jackal limbs with the others, and growl out your own anger and relief and sweet need, your raging unreasonable demands.

THE ROYAL BUTCHER

My father was a butcher; I'm a butcher's son. We hung the heavy carcasses on hooks together. That was a long time ago. My own children are scattered to other countries, other lives. I command a staff of dozens.

There are particular costs to a position like mine, particular accommodations one comes to make.

From time to time, the emperor's guards require my help with the disposal of some meat. Not so often, really. Once a year maybe, or twice.

I understand my role precisely.

I never ask what sort of animal it is for which we make these special arrangements.

NEIGHBORS

He was a drunk. Miles. He must be dead by now, because it's been years since I've seen him, and even then he showed no signs of letting up until he died. This is an important story, okay? I want you to see that. If we're going to have to share this room today, before and after, I want you to know this much at least.

He lived above me in this three-flat down by UIC, and some nights I'd hear him crawling up the stairs to his apartment, stopping to rest on my landing, crying, slamming his head against my door. He was always pushing his hair out of his eyes.

He didn't work, not really. He'd get a job for a few weeks, quit or get fired. I'm not sure how he paid his rent. He told me his family was rich, but I didn't know whether to believe him. Ever since school ended that spring, I'd been working as a parking lot attendant downtown, bent over in a tiny hut all day, making change for impatient people in nice cars. I hated their guts. I wore a stiff uniform shirt.

So they're going to come get me out of here in a minute, okay? The anesthesia first, and on down the hall to cut me open. But I've got enough time to really lay this out for you, I think. I think I do.

He was a racist, a bully. He pulled his pants down in bars. He got beat up a lot and I don't know why I even kept speaking to him, but I did. In some way, hanging out with him made me feel better about my own life.

He was the only person I told about losing my scholarship. My grades had been too low, I'd barely even made it a year. The concrete campus, crowds of students. I had tried, set my alarm every morning, but on a lot of days I just couldn't do it. I'd sit on the edge of my bed and stare at the carpet. I'd go to sleep again.

I told Miles. I hadn't even told my family yet—they all thought I was going back in the fall, that everything was fine. Miles laughed, he didn't care, he was a drunk, he told me a story about an ex-girlfriend of his who joined the Navy. The story didn't make any sense.

One of his jobs—it only lasted a few days—was to wear a lobster suit and pass out fliers. It was for a seafood place; the suit was ridiculous. Red rubber, with these huge claws extending four or five feet over his head. This was in summer. I think it paid minimum wage, standing in the sun all day in that suit, but Miles took the job. He thought it was funny.

He said the little lobsters chased him. Those are the words he used. They were kids—young kids, twelve or thirteen years old, killing some time downtown. I guess they were hassling him, making fun of the suit, and he slapped one of them, hard, and they chased him for blocks, throwing stones at him, bottles, anything they could pick up as they ran.

Even while he was telling me this, I knew there was no way it really happened. I just couldn't believe him—there was something fake about the whole thing—but why did he tell it to me? And who really beat him up in that lobster suit? Because it was the damn suit that did it, he said, that slowed him down. He said he could've escaped easily, or stopped to fight, but the suit got in the way. It was heavy and hot, and the claws fell into his face, made it hard for him to see. Sprinting, the claws bouncing. He said he tripped and fell and the kids kicked him in the back and legs. They surrounded him, landing blows from behind, always from behind, and he was drunk and out of shape and crying, this giant lobster spinning around.

For years in my mind I've come back to that lobster suit, that running. He said they stomped him through the heavy rubber. And I don't believe it happened, I don't, but it's like I was there anyway, like that was me. If this thing doesn't go right today, if I'm not back in here with you this afternoon, then at least you'll know this much about my life, okay? If anybody ever asks.

The kids got bored finally, I guess—they were just kids. Or whoever it really was.

Miles eventually made it home, and I drove him to the hospital to get stitches put in his head. He was still wearing the suit, the whole long drive in my car in the dark. When I asked about changing clothes, he sniffled and shouted and I didn't ask again.

You really have to be something to get everyone's attention in a big-city emergency room. You know that as well as anybody, right? From the second we walked through the sliding doors that night, though, the whole place was watching us. Nurses behind the counter, patients on plastic chairs. We walked across the room, side by side, the people staring.

A nurse gave him a form on a clipboard and I stood right there next to him while he filled it out. The red claws bounced above his head. His nose was running. He had smudges of dirt and dried blood on his forehead, his cheeks. The lobster suit was torn and dirty. He wouldn't stop crying. I turned around and faced the room. The rows of chairs, the crowd. They *gawked*.

You need to understand that I really didn't like this guy. I barely knew him, and what I did know was desperate and sad, ugly. If what he said was true, he'd slapped a kid half his size that afternoon. But it wasn't true, I don't think.

I was such a mess in those years. Lonely all the time and frightened. In pictures from then, I'm always hunched over, hair unwashed. I was so young. But that night—listen—that night I stayed right there with Miles, shoulder to shoulder. I brushed the dirt off him. I let the people look. And when the doctors had done their work, finally, I took him with me, back to where we lived.

THREE

THE TIGERKEEPER'S DAUGHTER

Famine—crops wither, cattle die. The emperor owns six white tigers. They eat enormous chunks of meat every other day. Their keeper watches them. He has a daughter, parents, who can blame him? He steals the meat and brings it home.

He does this again, then again. Word spreads. Soon, relatives begin to gather, and friends of relatives, and their relatives and friends. They stand silently in front of his hut. They hold infants in their arms, lead children by the hand. Some of them are sick. What choice is there? None. His daughter nods, she invites the weakest inside, they share the food.

Soon, the keeper is caught, of course—the tigers are suspiciously thin, their ribs visible. In his rage, the emperor orders him hurled into the tiger cage. The daughter turns her head away, her whole body shaking.

The famine continues. Food becomes still scarcer. Eventually, the emperor realizes he has no choice. The tigers are slaughtered and roasted. The emperor eats them from long platters.

Still the famine continues. One day, the villagers rise up. Carrying clubs and sharp knives, they storm the castle, searching for the rumored caches of food. There aren't any. The castle is bare—the shoes eaten, the curtains.

The villagers stab the emperor to death and leave his body on the floor. Hours later, a few of them return. They are desperate and starving. They build a fire and roast the body. They eat. One of them is the tigerkeeper's daughter.

She chews. She thinks of her father. It's hard for her to swallow. She remembers him turning toward her with a grin. The sharp line of his nose. She remembers the sound of his laugh, the powerful waves of it, his roaring.

EMPLOYEE

My job is, my job has been, to put the turnips into bags, but today—Jerry got a call from downtown, my boss Jerry. I'm not a dumb guy, okay? There's this whole politico-economic thing going on out here that I'm just a tiny part of, I get all that. But still. My back hurts from the scooping, my hands hurt.

Jerry says my job from now on is to put the turnips into sacks.

EVERY LIFE IS A PRIVATE LIFE

While the old man was dying, he cried out in his delirium. Names. The family gathered around, wept for him, for themselves. He called for his brother—dead so long. His mother. He called for his wife. And another name. They looked at each other.

Christine? She could be a girl from the second grade, or an old Sunday school teacher, or a mistress.

They all loved him. None of them knew.

Every life a private life.

Think on that.

Every life a mystery.

PLAN A/PLAN B

I went to school to be a grackle, you know, but nobody was hiring and I got a gig part-time as a paperweight. It's all right. You just push down, mainly—that's the key. Push down. Sometimes, though, through the windows, I see them out there in the swoop and the wheel of it and for a couple of minutes it's a little hard to breathe. Like what if I just let the papers go?

Just to see what the wind does with them.

To watch each sheet lift off and turn.

POOR, LONELY DONKEY

The donkey waits at O'Hare for a connecting flight, pacing the long, brightly lit airport terminals, their smooth floors. He stares at people.

The young women are more beautiful than before, he thinks—their hair, their hips and bellies, the utter mystery of how they stand, of how they pull their rolling suitcases behind them by long handles. They wear jeans or short skirts, T-shirts with animals on them. They wear sneakers, slacks, long thin jackets—he has to catch his breath. He does. This is the sexiest airport he's ever seen.

The flight is delayed.

He drinks coffee.

The donkey's hooves clatter as he walks from one terminal to another, cycles back. Is it really that they're more beautiful? Can that be possible? Or is it just that he looks more closely now—can *bear* to look more closely?

When he was young, the women were so bright, so terrifying. They overwhelmed. They hurt his eyes almost; he had to look away.

Or not. Maybe that's an exaggeration, maybe that's overstating it. Who can recall a thing like that clearly? It's been so long.

Anyway, it isn't only sexual, the donkey thinks, stepping onto one of those long moving sidewalks, it isn't, because the young men are more beautiful than they used to be, and the old men and the old women, the children, it's everyone, the miracle of their eyes and bodies, their hands making motions, their legs carrying them back and forth, the sinew and bone and clean skin, which doesn't mean it isn't sex, though, the donkey corrects himself, he's no fool, he's read Freud, he knows a little something about the massive surging power of subconscious drives—what difference does it make?

Dark eyes, light eyes, eyes close together, far apart, higher or lower, more or less deeply set in the skull. There isn't time to absorb a face, even begin to, before it's gone and another one coming toward him.

The flight is delayed still further. The donkey gets another cup of coffee, tries to read *The New York Times*. He turns the pages blankly, then folds the paper and tucks it beneath his seat. He stretches out his legs, pulls them back.

The older he gets, the more people he's seen. More every day. How many? Tens of thousands, hundreds of thousands, millions? He doesn't know. In one lifetime, how many knuckles do you see, how many eyelashes?

Maybe his plane is never leaving. Coming toward him is a tall woman with a sharp face, straight dark hair. Then a long-armed guy and a kid with flashing gym shoes.

He is impatient, as restless as he has been in his entire life. He is close to tears. Poor, lonely donkey.

He wants to be important. He wants to be embraced by strangers. If he could die for these people, he would, he thinks suddenly, sacrifice his donkey body that they might be saved. He pictures himself, racked and broken, hanging from a cross on a hilltop—and that's right, that's good, there it is, that's how much he wants to give.

He's pretty keyed up right now. He recognizes that. The Jesus thing is a little much, okay, but *something's* lifting in him.

An airport employee wheels an old woman past. She's wearing a dark brown shawl over her shoulders. A man in a cowboy hat, then a young fellow with long hair and headphones.

Again the donkey paces.

He really is a donkey. In some way, for as long as he can remember, he's known. The miracle of it—donkey born to human parents, donkey assuming human form. Many people in his life have not recognized this important fact, have not seen clearly, and even he, often, for long stretches, years at a time, has been able to deny his essential donkeyness, but now, today in this sex airport, he feels himself swelling toward a real understanding. There are so many ways to say this. In the beginning was the donkey, donkey made of song, of mud and dung and sunlight. What was his name then, before there were names? Old Donkey, First Donkey, Donkey Okay (beautiful and thin, going at those windmills.)

He watches the crowd in the airport. He has never been so happy.

Or maybe it's more like this. In the beginning, when the waters covered the face of the earth, the donkey floated in a rowboat. He had a small bird with him, and the donkey and the bird argued about who would do what and finally they drew straws and it came out the way it came out. Small bird would fly around, and Donkey, Old Donkey, Donkey

Okay—he would do the rest, assume various forms, would take on the shapes of airport commuters if required, would carry anything, anytime, no matter what, wherever there was a burden, that's just how the tasks were divided, just how it turned out. Fair and square. He would carry everything. And above him, always, small bird would dip and soar, make loops.

The crowds keep coming, pouring on and off the planes. A mother pushing a stroller, a man in turquoise sweatpants. Some sort of high school band on a trip.

His flight doesn't leave for a long time.

THE NEW BEAR

The new bear asks a question and the old bear considers. He sighs, exhales his cigarette smoke.

"The tutu. Yeah." He scratches the side of his face thoughtfully.

"Comfortable it isn't, I gotta tell you. But what are you gonna do? My pal Frank tried that King of the Animal World stuff a few years back and let's just say it didn't go over too well. Let's just leave it at that, if you know what I mean."

The new bear is swinging his large head back and forth. His mouth hangs slightly open. The old bear glances at him, continues.

"You have to make the best of it, that's where I'm coming from. The accommodations are all right, three meals a day. Shop around. It's not a bad deal. It could be a zoo for Christ's sake. Have you seen those cages? No privacy. Here you got afternoons off. Free and clear. Except on matinee days, of course. But otherwise yeah. Every afternoon. That's something to take into consideration at least. To have in mind."

He pauses again, leans back and crosses one leg over the other. He looks up at the ceiling and closes his eyes.

"It itches." Another drag on his cigarette.

"I'll be completely up-front with you, the tutu itches. It's going to rub your fur, and it's going to itch. There it is. But again, let's try to put things into perspective. What's a little itching? It's not the end of the world, am I right?"

The new bear mumbles something.

"Speak up, pal," the old bear says. He rocks forward, uncrosses his legs, and stubs the cigarette out in the ashtray. He looks around the cage. "Right out of the woods, some of them."

"I said, I don't know *how* to dance," the new bear mumbles again. He's shaggy, huge, maybe two or three years old.

The old bear roars. "Don't know how to . . .? Oh, that's rich." He snorts. "I wish Frank could've heard that one. Doesn't know how to dance. Oh, kid, that's priceless. Where did they find you?"

He shakes his head. "Of course you don't know how to dance." He looks around, stage whispers, "You're a *bear.*"

Sitting back again, chuckling, he fumbles for the pack, lights up. "None of us know how to dance when we get here, kid. That's why it's funny. That's the whole damn point. Otherwise . . ." He waves his cigarette in the air; smoke trails expansively. "Otherwise, it wouldn't make any sense, am I right?"

The new bear swings his head again. It lurches on the end of his neck like a wrecking ball.

"You'll pick it up, though." The old bear nods, lips pursed. "You're lucky you talked to me, kid. Some of these other guys . . ." He trails off. "Well, they just don't understand teaching, if you see what I mean. But me, I'll show you a few of the basics and you'll be in good shape. Nothing to worry about there." The new bear hesitates, but the old bear waves his paw, insisting, and gets out of his recliner with a grunt. He takes a last drag of his cigarette, crushes it out. He leans slowly to one side, then the other, stretching his back.

The two bears stand facing each other. The old bear is smaller, with shorter fur. He's got a belly. "Paws here." The old bear places the new bear's paw on his hip. "Okay. I'll let you lead on this one. Just keep the count going, *one* two three, *one* two three . . ." He puts a foot forward, backward, guides the new bear through the steps. They stride, turn clumsily, come back around.

"That's it, kid, you're getting it." The old bear's a little out of breath, but he doesn't stop, forward and backward, the two of them, turning, turning, *one* two three, *one* two three.

Some of the other bears have gathered to watch. "He's pretty good," someone calls out, and someone else whistles. The old bear pays no attention.

The new bear is concentrating, tongue sticking from the side of his mouth, but he's getting the hang of it, *one* two three, *one* two three, to an end of the cage and back, the two of them, dancing, picking up speed, moving smoothly now, in step, *one* two three, the whole cage watching, the whole cage starting to clap. Step, turn, glide, step back, and the old bear throws in a little shake of the hips like the old days, a little show-off wiggle for the crowd, and when he comes back in the new bear's right there with him, right in time, just like Frank would've been. Oh, it's been so long. There's something in the old bear's throat. They move together through another turn, bodies in motion, in rhythm, step step, just right, and the old bear tries a spin, what the hell, and they nail it, just the way it's supposed to go, come back, step again, turn . . . the old bear whispers, "Dip me."

And the new bear does.

THE GUEST

They're her friends, more or less. Her former boss and his wife. She's been a guest in their immaculate home on more occasions than she can count. And last night when she saw the piece of dog shit on the floor—right there by the piano—she didn't pick it up.

What is there to say about that house? It's enormous, high ceilings, a view of the bay. Paintings on the walls, shelves filled with books. The turd lay in a fat curve on the shining hardwood floor, and she could've picked it up in a paper towel, thrown it out. She could've told the housekeeper.

They have a housekeeper.

When she was a kid, she took a card to elementary school every day so she could get a free lunch. It was no big deal. A lot of kids at her school had one.

Does that explain it? Is that enough?

Should she say more? That in the small apartments of her childhood there were no books, no paintings on the walls? None of that is the fault of her friends. And she was happy as a kid, that's important. It was a happy childhood.

She likes to think that we don't carry our heavy history always across our shoulders, that the past will just stay back there where it belongs. But when she saw the shit on their floor, it thrilled her more than music. More than wild birds!

What if she squished it with her foot? Just smeared it on that floor? She took a quick step, another.

"There you are!" her friends called from the balcony, waving.

She was nearly breathless. She had to clear her throat before the words could come.

"Here I am," she agreed.

SOBRIETY

Say there's a game: you're walking by yourself on a dirt road through a forest at sundown, and all you have to do is keep walking. Nothing to it. One foot, then the other foot, then the other foot, forever, and the only thing you aren't allowed to do—even when the sun slips down behind the hills, even when the darkness thickens all around you, even when the devil starts his moaning in the trees—the only thing you *aren't* allowed to do is run.

TEACHING

Years going by, gone by, Butler High School with new buildings, the old ones demolished. Larger rooms now, and fresh paint. Lockers like soldiers in rows.

I'm a substitute teacher, first week on the job, rode over this morning on my bike, pushing hard along the frontage road with a clean shirt on. I was fourteen years old in this place. I was fifteen, I was sixteen, and now I'm all grown up. The sky's the same.

I should fall to my knees, rip my clothes and hair, but I don't. I say good morning and the kids swirl. I don't know any of them.

At lunch I wander the new hallways, stopping teachers to ask how long they've worked here. It's important, this search for someone who remembers me, and I find one woman who says she does. I don't remember her. We stare at each other.

All afternoon I watch kids' faces, skinny arms. I want to tell them what's coming—the brain's long howling, the way their lives will uncurl and flap, the way one of them, at least one, will kneel on the railroad tracks someday, high from sniffing paint, and beg the world to send a train. Maybe they already know, some of them. I didn't, not at their age, I don't think. It all happened later.

I need to tell them what's coming. I want to give them advice. I stand, swallow. Their eyes are on me. Love deeply, I say, and they look confused, not sure whether to crack up or be frightened. A chair scrapes the floor.

Take care of each other, I say.

Hold on, I say.

When the bell rings, they charge out of the room.

SIMPLE

Buenos Aires, 1979

The man is young, chubby, with a thick mustache hiding his upper lip, and he thrashes and shouts while the soldiers drag him to the car, *Avísenle a Nora Gutierrez—soy Wilson Gutierrez—que le avisen a Nora.* His voice is a rising squeal. The crowd eyes itself. Tonight, at home, some of these people will have trouble swallowing their food, they will snap at their families or turn silent for no reason, they will think about the man being dragged to the car and how terror crystallizes everything. The world gets so simple. Men with guns are taking him away, he wants someone to warn—is it his wife? his mother? Panicked, pitiful, he shouts his name and her name at strangers until the door slams and they tie the blindfold around his face. The people chew a hunk of bread or a mouthful of meat, there isn't enough saliva, they mash food in their jaws, chew, swallow. One woman remembers that the wind blew a sheet of newspaper along the curb while Wilson Gutierrez flopped his pudgy body in the soldiers' arms. A man remembers that the exhaust from the car—a dark Ford Falcon, they always drive Ford Falcons—spread along the pavement in a white cloud he knew meant some sort of engine trouble and he began to think that maybe it was time to paint his bathroom, and now he wants to know why, of all possible thoughts, that particular thought? He isn't a cruel or uncaring person, this man, he doesn't consider painted bathrooms more important than the lives of people, he is a supervisor six days a week in a factory that produces leather goods, he is liked, for the most part, by those who work under him, he has a wife, a son, three daughters, the youngest is named Beatriz, she takes piano lessons. The piano teacher has gray hair, she's tall. The man brings a fork to his lips, spicy sausage, oily and hot, steam rises, he is ravenous, never this hungry in his life, lowers his barely trembling hand, he blows on the food, pauses, blows again, puts the fork inside his mouth. So many more meals to get through, breaded beef, green salad with onion, ravioli, he must chew, swallow, look across the table, comment about work, another bite, keep chewing, smells of cigarettes and garlic, voices murmuring, traffic, thousands of meals to get through, one by one, just like this, he chews, he swallows, it's simple. Things could always be worse, they could be, he jerks his head around—at all the windows, sparrows.

BOOM-BOOM WHOOP

Lucy was trying to hold herself together. On days she couldn't do it, she went to the store and bought bacon, two thick pounds wrapped in cellophane. In the checkout line she wanted to shriek at the customers ahead of her, punch their heads, get them out of the way. They stood dopily—staring at nothing—then shuffled forward to pay and gather their supplies. They bought cereal in bright boxes; they bought bread, soup, detergent. The labels were cheerful and aggressive. Awful bouncy music came over the loudspeakers. Lucy breathed in and out, teeth clenched, suffering, getting through.

She drove home with her mouth watering and cooked the bacon in a pan, every single piece. She crammed the slices into her face. The crunch and salt in her mouth. The taste was so soft. It flooded in her, made her safe. She threw herself into chewing, swallowing. She ate until she was sick, her teeth and tongue coated in grease.

On days like that, Shannon could smell the bacon from their hallway. Lucy waited to hear her coming up the stairs. Shannon's feet in those clunky shoes she wore so her ankles wouldn't swell. Shannon's big arms and no-bullshit laugh. Lucy lay on the couch on her side, queasy, reeling. For hours she waited to hear Shannon's footsteps on the stairs. She shut her eyes. She organized all her thoughts around that waiting.

Since she'd first arrived in town, four weeks ago, Lucy had painted houses for a living, part-time. She'd found a boss who'd leave her alone, send her out by herself, not ask any questions. Shannon worked as a nurse at the main hospital downtown. There were six units in their apartment building, two to a floor, and Shannon and Lucy lived on top, across a narrow hallway from each other. In the trees below Lucy's window, sparrows had built their nests. Sunday, bacon-sick, Lucy watched birds hop along the branches. She'd crossed the hallway to Shannon's apartment three times and knocked, but there was no answer. Just silence through the door. Now she waited.

Sparrows hopped on branches. The radio talked to her for a while, but she turned it off. The windows of her apartment were clean; warm sunlight poured through the glass. She would have opened the windows, but they were painted shut with thick white paint, the brush marks still showing. She'd found them that way when she moved in and hadn't done anything about it. She had the thinner, of course, all the materials from work—but that was for work, she could force herself into action for work. At home, it was different. That morning it had taken her two hours to decide which sweatshirt to wear. She sat on the edge of her bed looking at them, paralyzed by them. A blue one, a gray one. Their empty arms hanging helplessly. How to choose? She wanted to weep. The collar on the gray one was beginning to fray, threads coming apart, a slight opening in the seam.

Who would have thought she'd end up in New Mexico? Who would've thought her own clothes could derail her like this? Finally, she'd made herself put on the blue sweatshirt. Now she made herself wash the greasy pan, the dishes. Water so hot her hands swelled with blood. She put the leftover bacon into the garbage along with the Styrofoam and wrap, and took the bag down the stairs to the large bin behind the building. Back inside, concentrating on not puking, she sat at the kitchen table. The wallpaper had tiny green flowers on it. Every few inches, the pattern repeated the same flower. It was something she'd never noticed before.

Lucy started a list about herself in her mind, a sing-song, delicate list. She wasn't starving, she wasn't cold, she wasn't sleeping outside. She had all her limbs, she could see, she had clothes to wear, money in her checking account, a little money. No one was throwing rocks at her, no one was kicking her.

The list was supposed to help, but it didn't. It was supposed to convince her that she had nothing to complain about. It was supposed to ward off self-pity. She started the list again.

Finally, near evening, Shannon came home. Shannon came home and Lucy met her in the hallway. "I'm not doing so good today," she said.

Shannon turned her head sideways. "What's going on?"

"Just bad," Lucy said, and bit her lip.

Shannon was tired. Lucy wasn't someone she knew that well. She hesitated for a moment. "If you don't want to be by yourself," she said, "you can come on with me to my cousin's house." She looked Lucy up and down. "Come on with me," she said. "They won't mind."

Shannon changed clothes quickly, talking to Lucy the whole time from the bedroom. Lucy stood in the kitchen. Shannon's refrigerator was covered with pictures, held on by magnets in silly shapes—a corn cob, a tiny pig with a curly tail, a woman with beehive hair, a pickup truck. The pictures were all of people Lucy didn't know. She didn't know anyone in this town, she thought. Again she wanted to weep. Martín's horse-face, his slow stupid body. After that first time she left him and came back, he began to clamp his hands around her thin wrists like handcuffs. He'd lean in toward her, face shiny with panic, make her promise she'd never leave again. Shannon, calling from the other room, said that tonight was a barbecue for her cousin's birthday, and she was late already, and maybe if Lucy came along Lucy would be able to distract the family so they didn't kill Shannon.

She laughed at that, laughed at her own joke like she always did, and came into the kitchen in her jeans. "Come on then," she said, and touched Lucy's arm. Lucy let herself be led down the stairs and outside to Shannon's pickup.

"Thanks for this," she told Shannon, but Shannon had turned the radio on, loud, and was looking over her shoulder to back the truck down their narrow driveway. Shannon was already moving on to the next thing.

In traffic, Lucy put on her seat belt. Shannon sang along to the radio.

The list continued—Lucy wasn't in a hospital. She didn't have cancer, she didn't have AIDS, she didn't have leprosy. She could talk, no one had cut off her tongue. She could feel it, her tongue, a thick wet slug in her mouth. There were people in the world who'd had a tongue cut off. Lucy was telling herself that.

At the end of the block, Shannon turned onto a larger street. It was getting dark—every few blocks someone's twin headlights flicked on. They drove past a series of take-out restaurants, a laundromat, a school.

Then the highway. Shannon wove from lane to lane, jabbed constantly at the buttons on her radio to find a better song. The huge eighteen-wheelers had yellow lights along their sides. When one of the trucks was next to them, Lucy held her breath. She didn't trust that something so large wouldn't just swerve into them, or topple, send them sliding into the guardrail, hammer Shannon's tiny pickup flat.

"You'll like my cousin Charlie," Shannon said, "she's a trip."

Shannon knew she was pushing. She was trying to get at Lucy. This singing along, this chatter. That's what she did with her patients at the hospital. You acted as if you were oblivious to pain, as if it just weren't there, you chatted about the ballgames, you laughed loud and deep at everything. It energized them, dragged them back to the surface. It was what the sick and the suffering required of Shannon. It was what she provided for them.

"Thirty-five or thirty-six or some shit," Shannon went on, explaining. "A few years older than me anyway. I couldn't stand her when we were kids. Man. But she went and got cool when I wasn't paying attention. She's a trip."

They exited the highway, Lucy pale and concentrated. Her insides seemed slick to her, bacon-greased, and the jolting of the pickup was unsettling. She felt a button growing in the back of her throat, a nodule, a tiny latch. She squeezed her eyes into slits and tried not to let the latch give way, but at the red light of the access road, suddenly, it was too late. She shoved the passenger door open and threw up in a rush— flecks of grease and meat. She paused, threw up again. The buck of her body, refusing. Mouth stretched wide. Taste of bacon. Cars were passing them.

Shannon turned off the radio with a click. "I'm going to pull off the road, honey," she said. Her voice was calm. "Close the door for a second."

Lucy ran her tongue over her teeth, spit thickly, brought the door toward herself, and Shannon maneuvered across the lanes and onto the shoulder. Shannon lifted a handkerchief from her purse and got out. "Okay," she said. "Okay, Lucy."

She walked around the loud front of her truck and pulled open Lucy's door. She wiped her neighbor's chin and mouth, brushed the hair from her neighbor's clammy forehead. "Okay," she kept saying. This was another thing that was required of her. She cleaned people up and told them okay. She was good at it.

When Shannon and Lucy got there, the party was in full swing. The front door was propped open and a crowd was talking and laughing on the porch. A roar went up when Shannon climbed the steps, and she was hugged and prodded and shouted at in greeting. She introduced Lucy quickly— "This is Lucy, don't mess with her"—and pushed into the house. Lucy trailed behind, helpless, her mouth sticky. Music swelled through the rooms; people stood in little clumps. They walked through the house to the backyard where they were greeted by Charlie and a whole series of other cousins who immediately blurred together in Lucy's head, all looking vaguely alike, big, loud women with round faces, small eyes, huge grins. Shannon's mother was there, too, a small, bent woman who stood over the meat hissing and dripping on the grill. She jabbed at it with a metal spatula.

After she threw up, Lucy apologized again and again to Shannon, who ignored her. "Stop that," she said finally. "There's a birthday party to get to."

And there they were. Lucy sat in a lawn chair at the edge of the crowd. She was calm—a calmness that came from exhaustion. She felt limp, wrung-out. She reviewed the list of all the ways she wasn't suffering. She watched Shannon move and talk.

In the bathroom, Lucy used someone's bright orange toothbrush, found mouthwash, swished it around. It foamed in her mouth. She looked at the cabinets. Two mirrored doors. Her thin bird-face staring back, circles under the eyes. Inside the cabinet, she found dental floss and flossed hard, which she hadn't done in a long time. Her gums bled. She threw away the floss, swished more mouthwash, brushed again.

She wanted to keep looking—sometimes the things you find in medicine cabinets will make your jaw drop—but she didn't. She went outside, sat again in the lawn chair. If she sucked at her gums, she could taste a little rust, some blood left over. She moved her tongue along the hard row of her teeth.

Shannon had been drinking and now she was bossing people around. She had told Charlie that she, Shannon, didn't like Charlie's husband, never had. She insisted that one song, a loud electronic dance mix, be played over and over, and shouted when someone tried to turn it off in the middle. The boom-boom of the song, the whoop. How could she ever explain how perfect it was? It loosed something wild and flooding in her throat. It made her want to move.

She looked over at Lucy sitting in the lawn chair. Lucy hadn't talked to anyone all night. Shannon wished Lucy would buck the hell up, would stand up and get over herself. She was so tired of taking care of people.

"You," she shouted, pointing at Lucy. "You need to buck the hell up."

Lucy smiled timidly.

Shannon laughed. What else could you do but laugh? Still, though, in her throat—that feeling the music brought, an abandon. She was restless, on the edge of something. She threw her hands in the air and moved to her mother, who was wiping the grease from the grill. Everyone had eaten.

"So," Shannon said. "Mom. How you been?"

Her mother looked aggrieved, nervous. Her gray hair was pulled back from her forehead, tied with an elastic band, and it escaped into a frizzy halo around her sharp face. She wore a man's plaid shirt over a faded blouse. "I've always enjoyed birthday parties," she said.

Already, there was something argumentative in her mother's voice. As if someone had accused her of not liking birthday parties, of being against them. Wanting to have them banned.

"I mean it," Shannon's mom insisted. "This birthday." She held the grill in one hand and wiped at each bar sloppily with a white rag. "Did I tell you about the birthdays at that parking garage?" Shannon didn't answer. Her mother kept going. "At the building downtown. Did I tell you?"

"How do I know?" Shannon said. "Am I supposed to keep track of every single thing you say?" She sat down.

"I wouldn't want to repeat myself," her mother said, and stopped wiping the grill. She grinned, a surprising flash of teeth. It changed her whole face, made her look calmer, less angry. Made her look younger.

"Tell it," Shannon waved her arm over her head, ran her hand over her own face. It felt soft under her palm. "Tell me. We've got time." She leaned back, crossed her legs at the ankle, tried to appear relaxed. That moment when her mother smiled—it was as if another person had peeked out from behind the curtain of her face, then jerked away. The music from inside was quieter now, somebody had put on a ballad, high trumpet in the background. Schmaltz. Strain of the slow Spanish melody. Like something pent-up, trapped, trying to push out through the trumpet's clear bell.

"Across the street from the prison," Shannon's mom began, but Shannon interrupted. "Lucy," she called. "Lucy, come over here!"

Lucy stood. "Bring that chair," Shannon told her, and when Lucy brought it over, she pointed and said, "Sit. We're going to hear a story." She laughed, loud, waved to her mother to go on. Her mother put the grill down, looked around, wiped her hands with quick strokes on the rag. It was an old T-shirt, Lucy saw, with black stripes of grease from the grill. Shannon's mom nodded to Lucy. These pale little girls her daughter brought around. There was no end to them. They made her think of starving little kittens. Mewling. Half-drowned. Fighting in some sack.

"For a time in Chicago," she explained to Lucy, "I had a job across the street from a prison." How long since she'd even thought about this? The tall, slender prison—the memory so clear! On the top floor was an exercise yard, and you could see right into it. "From where I worked," she told the young women, "one could see the prison, through the windows." She cleaned the offices—mopped, vacuumed, polished desks and tabletops, while the men in the exercise yard paced their constant, furious circles. Round and round. She had a cart with cleaning supplies, their sharp smell, and she pushed it from room to room, back to the elevator, again room to room, again the elevator, first floor to twelfth floor, every evening and all day Saturday, those years when Shannon was small.

Shannon's mother pulled another chair toward herself and sat, looked around, wiped her hands now on her shirt. The three women formed a triangle, just out of range of the lights from the house and the back porch. The rag on the grill shone in the dark.

Lucy didn't know this story would be about prison. Not fair. She was thinking now, forced to think now, about her own humiliating hours of it, of jail. Hot shame inside her mouth. This was just before she packed up and moved, barely more than a month before. She'd been drinking, and who could blame her for that, twenty-seven years old, everything falling apart? DWI on the way home, and no one—no one—

to pick her up. Waiting all night and through the morning for her mom, who never came, who said she'd had enough. Dry, bitter, sandpaper voice. Raw memory. Lucy sanded at herself with her mother's voice—"I've just had enough"—her own mother.

"Sometimes the prisoners would throw papers out of the windows of their cells, notes they had written, and there were young men down at the bottom waiting to pick them up. Every so often, pieces of paper would float down."

Lucy, listening, was trying to tell herself how lucky she was not to be a prisoner throwing notes to someone outside. She wasn't freezing to death, she wasn't in a hospital, things could be so much worse. Shannon's mom had her head tilted to the side, concentrating on her story—and Shannon wasn't buying a single word. No way. She bit her lip. "Come on now. They just let them open their windows up? In prison?" Her frustration was building. She felt like letting go, like giving in to whatever it was that flooded in her, catching in her throat when she heard her song—her perfect song—and this story of her mother's, made-up, going nowhere, it blocked her. The little jaunt down memory lane. The reminder of the jobs her mom had to take—the constant reference to sacrifice.

"I think so." Her mother's voice was precise, wounded. "Yes, or perhaps they pushed the paper through the edges. I don't know."

She took a drink. "Well." She paused, fussily, but Shannon didn't say anything. Shannon curled her toes in her shoes, uncurled them, willed herself to be patient. Forced herself. Lucy held her hands in her lap. One of the women in Lucy's cell that night had been in her sixties, missing teeth.

"I cleaned the offices," Shannon's mother went on. "And from the building where I worked, one could look out and see the prison, and a parking garage next door." She spoke slowly. Trying to get each word right. The smell of the cleaning supplies in their bright plastic bottles. Sharp. The shining surfaces, and outside, through the windows, the family on the roof, napkins blowing away, the prison building a needle into the sky. How to explain it?

She tried. "Sometimes," she began, "a family would drive up onto the roof of the parking garage with balloons and signs and . . . different cakes. The signs said 'Happy Birthday,' or someone's name."

The young women were looking at her. She kept trying. "They would bring the children, and even card tables. And sit down and have cake, right there on the roof, so he could see them, whoever he was, through his prison window. And he could celebrate with them."

Shannon thought she might just shake out of her skin. She couldn't listen to this, not now. She snorted, finally, the snort she'd been holding back, "Come on, Mom. That's just not true."

Her mom flinched, held her palms out, "I saw it."

"Come on now."

"I saw it. Happy birthday." She laughed suddenly, her voice turning hard. "That's all the birthday you get!"

Lucy and Shannon and Shannon's mother sat in silence for a moment. Lucy was thinking about prisons, about sending messages floating down on the air. She was trying to remember the last time she'd felt close to anyone at all. After she realized her mom really wasn't coming, she had called Martín. He was the only one she could think of. His smug leer, fake helpfulness. He lectured her the whole way home, and she sat silently—unshowered, forced to listen. No options. He took a long route on purpose, just to give himself more time to talk.

Shannon's mom asked if they would like anything else to drink. Shannon wanted another beer, Lucy, barely hearing the question, said she was fine. Was she fine? Shannon's mother made her way to the back porch.

"Well," Shannon said. "That's my mom."

"She seems really nice," Lucy said. Shannon patted her on the knee, an automatic gesture. "Yeah, well," she said. "How far does nice get you?"

Lucy wasn't paying attention. Shannon laughed for some reason. The night was clear, stars out above them in vivid and indifferent constellations. The music was off now, and there was the murmur of talk from inside, someone squealing.

The day after Lucy got out of jail, she ran. Just went, crossed state lines, she couldn't even think about how to start taking care of the mess she'd created. She hadn't talked to her family since she left, not to anyone from home. Every day that passed just made things worse, didn't it? In terms of the law and everything? But she couldn't get herself to do anything about it. Didn't even know where to begin. The weeks ground by. She wasn't paralyzed, she reminded herself of that. She wasn't buried alive, she wasn't drowning in the sea. That was something. Her body wasn't being held down by soldiers.

After a while, Shannon's mother came back with her drink, ice and liquor in a white plastic mug with a football helmet logo on it. She handed Shannon her beer. "Here you are," she said, and sat. She shifted her weight. The party seemed to be breaking up. A car door slammed.

"So, Charlie says they've been talking to you about moving and all, is that right?" Shannon played with the label on her bottle, picking lines into it with her thumbnail. If she closed her eyes, if she stood and danced barefoot in a circle, would it grow, that feeling in her throat? Would it swell? Lucy had her hands in her lap.

Shannon's mother sipped her drink. A sudden, bitter anger welled up in her. "I'm getting old," she said to Lucy and slapped her knee, sloshing a little bit of her drink over the edge of the plastic mug. "You get old and they throw you away!"

"Stop it," Shannon said, her voice sharp. Lucy flinched. Shannon took a breath deep into her lungs, held it a minute. Shannon's voice was the one people use when they're talking to their pets, Lucy thought, when they're giving orders.

"You get old," Shannon's mother said again. She drew her mouth tight. "And then they throw you away."

Shannon shook her head, reached over and touched her beer bottle to her mother's mug. "No one's throwing anyone anywhere and you know it," she said. She was trying to be reasonable. "You have to cut that out." She drank from her bottle, cold in her mouth, and after a moment, her mother drank, too. Picking again at her label, Shannon thought suddenly that this woman had seen her whole life. All of it. She remembered coming home from school to find her mom in the kitchen, in the small backyard.

Lucy wanted to ask Shannon's mother something about her prison story. Whether it was true, whether she'd tell it again, whether she ever read any of those notes, what they said. How could she not run downstairs and grab one, read it, see what was scribbled on it? Wouldn't you need to do that? She started to ask more than once, but each time she stopped herself. Shannon had another swallow of beer and leaped to her feet, shouted "Ha!" and gave her mother a clumsy hug. Her arm looped down around her neck, and her mother bent up, surprised. Hot whiskey-smell of her breathing. Shannon pressed her cheek against the older woman's wiry hair.

For a moment, tangled together like that, neither of them moved; then, embarrassed, Shannon's mother shoved her away. Shannon sat again in her chair, not looking at her mom or at Lucy. She studied the sky. "Mom," she said, and her mother muttered something that neither of the other women could hear.

"Mom," Shannon said again.

The woman looked at her daughter and the daughter made a sudden motion as if to throw beer on her. Explosive—flicking the wrist, pulling back at the last second, spilling foam. Shannon's mother flinched, blinked. The look on her face! Oh, for a moment, Shannon almost really did it, threw her beer bottle at her. Selfish selfish selfish, the way she never listened to anybody, wouldn't let anyone hug her. Her stories that went nowhere. It would serve her right, it really would.

Without warning, Lucy gasped once and hunched over in her chair. Her hands were balled into fists. "Did you ever read those notes?"

They both turned to her. Shannon looked back at her mother. Lucy's voice was way too loud, accusing. "Did you? From the prison?"

Shannon's mom shook her head. "What? I was at work."

Lucy breathed in and out, licked her rough lips. Taste of salt. "But what if it was important?"

"What?"

Lucy thought about her own mother's voice—"I've just had enough."

"Listen," Lucy said, "they couldn't get out, and they had something to say, and somebody . . ." The blood rushed to her face. "Somebody should've gone to listen."

Shannon's mom looked at her daughter, back at her daughter's friend. "I was at work," she said again. "Really." She turned her head sideways. "What?"

Shannon laughed a high, bitter laugh. "It's just a story, Lucy. Not even true, is it, Mom?"

"It's true," Shannon's mother said, standing. "Of course it's true." The way the papers floated down on the air, the signs on the parking garage roof.

"Come on," Shannon began—but Lucy interrupted her, "Oh, it's true."

"What?" Shannon's mother said. What was this girl talking about? Her daughter's starving kitten friend, what did she mean?

Shannon had her hand on Lucy's knee, her voice soft. She was taking control. Calm, forced herself to be calm. "It's okay, Lucy," she whispered. "It's okay." Her mother shook her head, sputtered.

"Those notes," her mom said. "They were from criminals." She looked around wildly, as if expecting to see a criminal right there in the yard, someone she could point to. A bank robber or something. A demonstration.

Lucy wished she hadn't said anything. She wished she hadn't come tonight with Shannon, wished she'd never gotten to this town. For a moment, she missed, somehow, really missed Martín, his stupid beautiful horse-face, his arrogance, his thoughtless cruelty. His hands clamped tightly around her thin wrists. At least that was familiar, that life, it was hers, she could recognize it. Who were these people here? This mother, this daughter? In the car, driving her home from jail, Martín had gone on and on about responsibility. She should've ripped out his eyes.

"I'm going inside," Shannon's mother announced.

"Mom," Shannon stood, gave her another hug, felt her bones through the thick plaid shirt. Stubborn, selfish woman. When Shannon was a little girl, the two of them would climb together up onto the roof of their house, just like that, no ladder or anything.

Shannon's mom let Shannon hold onto her for a moment, then struggled free. "Okay," Shannon said, and reached with the side of her knuckle to touch her mother's cheek. "Let's go in."

Lucy stood. She shouldn't have asked about the notes, shouldn't even be in this town. Mistakes piled too high to see over. The three of them crossed the yard and went in the back door. It swung and closed. In the kitchen, Charlie and her husband, a few others, were talking and laughing. Shannon's mom stalked through the kitchen and into the living room; Shannon and Lucy stayed beside the fridge.

First, Shannon's mom would lift her onto her shoulders and from there Shannon could climb to the angled red roof of the neighbor's toolshed, rough on her bare knees, warm. Her mom would pull herself up next and together they would scramble over to the roof of their house. One leg, then the other one. It was flat up there, high above everything. They were together. They could see the cars on the highway, the clouds, the houses spreading to the base of the mountains.

In the living room, Shannon's mother was sitting on the couch. Her legs sprawled in front of her. She was exhausted. Too tired to breathe anymore, to think. The story she told the two young women, the way they didn't understand how it was. How it was to push the cart of cleaning supplies from room to room, the smell of the elevators, the trudge of it.

One of the cousins had turned the music down. Shannon's mother raised herself up and pushed the hair from her forehead. "Turn it up," she shouted. "Don't you know this is a birthday party?" They couldn't get a single thing right without her. They really couldn't. "Turn it up!"

Shannon and Lucy stayed in the kitchen for a long time, not talking. Finally they said their goodbyes. Shannon's mom hugged Shannon, shook Lucy's hand. On the highway, Shannon drove fast. Lucy had drawn her knees to her chest. Lucy was young, she was healthy, she wasn't in prison. She wasn't locked in a cell somewhere, in solitary. There were no soldiers or guards to beat her, or worse. If she were, though—high up in a tiny room by herself, no escape—what would she ever write on a slip of paper? What message would she push out a window? And to whom?

Back at Charlie's house, in the living room in the dark, Shannon's mom was waiting for someone to come and take her home. The party was over. The air seemed to hum a little.

Shannon turned on the radio and punched the buttons. She wove from lane to lane, exited, stopped at a red light. She reached over automatically to pat Lucy on the knee. It wasn't Lucy's fault, poor thing.

Shannon was thinking that there was just no rest ever, no pause to her life. Her head was fuzzy with beer. She jabbed at the radio's buttons. Something happened, and then something else, and there was never time to react completely, to absorb it, before the world skittered on, tilted away. Beside her, Lucy stared through the windshield.

They were getting close to home when Shannon found the song, her song, the one she'd played over and over at the party. She shouted at the coincidence—turned the volume up, looked over at her neighbor—and the pickup slid right out of its lane. Jolted over the curb. Shannon gripped the wheel. Tires bounced. They were in a parking lot, oh here it came. Moving too fast. She turned hard one way, then the other. They nearly tilted. Lucy yelled to look out, but it was too late, no, wreck was coming, they were headed right for the side of a small flatbed truck piled high with watermelons—she tightened herself for the impact. The truck hit. Lucy's hands were up in front of her face and—the truck smashed, lurched, rolled on. Lucy's eyes were closed. She held her face with her hands. They were still moving. Shannon was trying to think. She looked down at her body, looked over at Lucy. Everything fine. Okay. Neither of them was hurt. They didn't hit that hard. No blood. She breathed out sharply. They weren't hurt. She started laughing—really laughing, a roar that came up from her belly. She couldn't stop it. The pickup still rolled through the parking lot. She turned the windshield wipers on for no reason, honked the horn. She looked over her shoulder at the mess.

She was laughing like a crazy woman. Tears in her eyes. The watermelons had bounced off each other in all directions, rolled into the street. Cars swerved around them, or smashed them. Rinds popped. Watermelon—what a ridiculous thing—in slippery pieces all over the pavement. Crushed. The music kept going boom-boom-boom.

Shannon's mother was still sitting in the dark, waiting for her ride. Just a few more minutes. She was thinking about her whole life. If she spread it out below her, what would it look like? The way the years slotted into each other. Did the pieces make a whole? Did they? She thought of those flimsy, crooked houses she and Shannon used to build with toothpicks and glue. Sometimes they would paint them in bright colors. Purple, orange, green. They'd throw them away.

The truck came to a stop, finally. Shannon was looking over her shoulder. In the street, someone got out of a car, then someone else. A voice shouted, but with the radio so loud, Shannon couldn't hear what was said, or even who said it. Lucy's face was shocked, wide-eyed. "Watermelons!"

Shannon wiped her own eyes, she couldn't stop laughing—it poured out of her.

One of the men who'd gotten out of a car was jogging toward them slowly. Shannon rolled the window down through her tears, reached to turn off the radio. The song disappeared. Engines, voices. A horn honked.

"Are you all right?" the man yelled, slowing to a walk. Back by the cars, people milled around. Broken chunks of watermelon lay everywhere. Another horn. "Hey," the man called again, "are you all right?"

They were all right. Oh. They were. "Shannon," Lucy said, "let's go." She meant it. Shannon caught her breath. She lifted her arm at the man. The laughter hadn't left. It was still there, just under the surface. Shannon could feel it. She swallowed, but when she looked again, the man in the parking lot was staring down at his shoes. He had one foot in the air.

"Aww," he said, a long, slow whine. "It's on my shoes."

Shannon burst. She opened her mouth wide and the laughter roared up from her belly. "Let's just go," Lucy said again, and Shannon reached for the radio, turned it even louder than before. The beat was thumping, necessary. It filled the cab. Hooting, Shannon put the pickup into gear, turned the steering wheel hard. They bounced out of the lot, pulled into traffic, the tires squealing a little, but they'd only gone a block and a half before she had to stop. She was laughing til she was half blind. She pulled the truck weakly to the side of the road. Music pounded. She hit the wheel with her hand. "On my shoes!" As if it were *possible* to live without smearing your shoes. As if anyone could, ever, under any circumstances. It crashed over her. Watermelon on a pair of shoes, wrecking them! She gasped for air. Those poor dumb shoes. It was overwhelming, more than she could explain. More than she could make room for. Her sides ached. She bent to the steering wheel, palm against the cool windshield . . . and Lucy was so far past exhausted that her body felt weightless. Floating. She couldn't think. The music didn't stop. She was touching her neighbor on the elbow . . . the bone there under the skin . . . wanting to speak, unsure . . . the actual bone there beneath the skin—

"Time to leave," Shannon's mom said brightly when Charlie's husband came into the room. Her voice broke. Oh. She bit her lip, stood, smoothed the front of her blouse with her hand. He followed her into the hall, out the front door to the porch—

"Hey Shannon, it's okay," Lucy said finally.

LUCY'S DREAM OF A FOREST

She can't remember it clearly in the morning. But she was a forest, in a way that made perfect sense. She wasn't *in* a forest, man. She *was* a forest—slick moss on her tree trunks—and it was wonderful.

LUCY'S DREAM OF HORSES

One of the horses is Martín. Martín inside a horse. She's trying to feed him sugar cubes from her palm, like she's read in books about girls who own horses doing. She's never had a horse. Martín is impatient with her, tossing his head. He doesn't want any fucking sugar cubes.

SIMPLE

Buenos Aires, 1979

The soldiers' car has accelerated away. The morning closes around the wound. The man has shouted to warn Nora, so all right, you heard him, you're a good person, some sort of saint, you choose to act, you will do this for a stranger, you will warn her.

But how many Nora Gutierrezes must there be in a city this size? How will you even begin to find the right address? And finding the address—how decide to walk to the bus stop?

And whether to climb the stairs, to knock on the door? How to know if Nora will answer? And if she answers, her face pale—what then?

"Yes?" she asks. Her hands are buried in her apron pockets, her mouth is anxious and small.

"Yes, what is it?"

THE ROOSTER IN THE THORNS

Once there was a rooster who lived with three hens in a coop on a farm in a grassy valley. Sometimes at night, while the hens slept, a fox would come and circle the coop, nose to the ground. He probed the wood and wire for weakness. "Pretty chickens," the fox whispered through the wire, "pretty rooster."

His voice rasped out of the darkness. On his perch, the rooster shivered and remained silent.

"Pretty," hissed the fox.

The nights when the fox came were frightening, but afterwards, in the clear mornings, every time, the rooster strutted around and crowed his lungs out. It was a kind of victory, an assertion of himself. In the sunshine, he bustled and scratched and argued with the hens. They clucked at him. During the day, the fox seemed like a dream, distant and insubstantial. At night, though, when the fox returned, he was flesh and blood, realer than anything. His smell made the rooster dizzy.

One evening, in a furious storm, the wind knocked over one of the coop's wooden poles—it just tore right out of the mud and sagged—and the rooster, shivering on his perch, knew that soon the fox would find his way in. Without saying anything to the sleeping hens, he slipped down from his perch and wiggled out of the coop.

In the rain he searched for a place to hide, and finally found a thorn bush. The thorns caught his feathers, scratched him, made him bleed, but he burrowed his way into their very center. He stood there, soaking wet, as the rain kept coming down and the wind blew. He was scared.

A little before dawn, the rain let up, and the rooster could see the stars. That's when the fox came. "Pretty chickens," the fox whispered. "Pretty rooster."

The hens clucked and shivered, shifting position on their perch. Soon, the fox found the broken place in the coop.

The noises were awful, the hens shrieking, the fox growling. From the thorn bush, the rooster listened. Why hadn't he warned them? Why hadn't he brought them along when he escaped?

The fox killed all three of the hens. The floor of the coop was a mess of blood and feathers. Then it was dawn.

Like an itching behind his eyes, the rooster felt the urge to crow. He stood hunched over and tiny in the middle of the thorn bush, still soaking wet. He could see the fox gnawing on the body of one of the hens.

The rooster had crowed every morning of his life. It was like holding back a sneeze, or an orgasm. He closed his eyes and swallowed. He held himself as tense as a guitar string, vibrating there in the middle of the thorn bush, trying not to crow.

The fox ate two of the hens right there in front of him. The rooster saw it happen. The third hen, the fox trotted away with. The rooster hadn't crowed—the first dawn of his entire life that he hadn't crowed.

The man came, finally, cursing. He shook his head and called his wife. She shook her head. In the thorns, the rooster was exhausted. His eyes felt glued open. That afternoon, he slept, a little, and dreamed of the fox. In a blur of motion, the fox tore the hens.

Night fell, cold and clear. The rooster was hiding in the thorn bush. He had no plan. His mind was blank. The fox came.

The fox nosed around the coop, nosed around the thorn bush. The ground was still muddy. The fox went away, but returned just before dawn. The rooster could see him sitting on a rise behind the coop. The rooster did not crow. If he crowed, the fox would find him. So the rooster let the sun rise without crowing—the second dawn in his life that he hadn't crowed.

Again, the rooster passed the day shivering in the middle of the thorn bush. He drank a little rainwater that had puddled around his feet, but soon that dried. He ate some thorns. He slept for a few minutes. He jerked awake.

That night, again the fox came, his nose to the ground. "Pretty rooster," he whispered, "pretty rooster."

Just before dawn, the rooster could see the fox sitting on the rise behind the chicken coop. The rooster didn't crow—the third dawn of his life that he hadn't crowed.

The woman found him that morning. She pulled back the branches of the thorn bush and lifted him out. She gave him food and water, shook her head, called her husband. Her husband shook his head. In the afternoon, he repaired the coop. Inside, the rooster sat on his perch and shivered. A little blood was still on the ground.

The rooster slept fitfully that night. He woke with a start. The fox was there, outside the coop. "Pretty rooster," the fox whispered. The rooster felt as if his perch were tilting, as if he would fall off any moment. He gripped it tightly with his feet. The fox crept around the coop, probing for weaknesses, and, finally, he went away.

In the morning, the sun rose. The rooster was too tired to crow. He watched the dawn dumbly. The light spread across the enormous sky.

Those days. They must have passed, they must have had mornings and afternoons and evenings and nights. Later, the rooster won't remember them clearly. He must have eaten food, drunk water. He doesn't know. He knows he gripped his perch. He slept in fits and snapped awake at the slightest sound. Every time he woke he was disoriented for a few moments, unable to recognize his surroundings. He jerked his head around to see the danger. He had the feeling, always, that there was something right behind him. He was scared to stay on the perch and he was scared to leave the perch. He gripped it hard.

After a few days, some other chickens arrived—bustling hens, a young, strutting rooster. The man tossed them in the coop and the rooster in the coop instantly flew at them, pecking and beating them with his wings. He attacked furiously, all of them at once. It wasn't something he thought about, he just did it. He knocked them down, he pecked at their eyes, he was shouting. The young rooster knocked him right off his feet, sent him rolling in the dirt and then stood over him, threatened him, asked him what the hell his problem might be, but the rooster on the ground didn't move. He had his eyes closed. He was waiting for the young rooster to kill him, but that didn't happen.

Later that afternoon, some of the hens tried to engage him in conversation. They had questions for him, about the coop, the people. The rooster opened his beak to speak, but nothing came out. He couldn't make a sound. After a few minutes, the hens quit trying.

For the most part, the new arrivals ignored the old rooster. They thought he was crazy. Sometimes he would rush the young rooster, pecking and shouting, and the young rooster would knock him down into the dirt. They all got used to it eventually.

Every morning, the young rooster greeted the dawn with his lusty crows, but the old rooster, the rooster who had hidden himself in the thorns, who had not warned the hens about the fox—he never crowed. During the day, he would spend most of his time on his perch, though when the sun was shining he would sometimes come down and scratch a little in the dirt. For the most part, he didn't talk, though once in a while he would start in on one of the hens. "Pretty chicken," he'd coo, "pretty, pretty." He'd stalk after her, everywhere she went in the coop. "Pretty," he'd whisper, "So pretty." He'd do this until the young rooster, fed up, would come over and knock him down, roll him in the dirt, tell him to cut it out for the love of God, you creepy old bird. The old rooster would laugh then, lying in the dirt at his young assailant's feet. Laugh helplessly, close to tears. Disgusted, the young rooster would shake his head and walk away.

Occasionally the fox would come around, or maybe it was another fox. It would whisper into the coop, and the brash young rooster would respond. "Just try it," he'd say, "just you try it." The hens clucked, impressed. When this happened, the old rooster flew at the young one, tried to peck out his eyes. More than anything else in the world, he wanted to leave him with scabbed-over empty eye sockets, just to show him. Show him what? He didn't know. The young rooster knocked him down into the dirt.

Spring turned into summer. The days were longer and hotter.

In the coop, the hens were having the same conversation as always.

"Are you hungry?" said one.

"Yes," said the other.

"Let's scratch in the dirt."

"Yes, let's scratch in the dirt."

This shit drove the rooster crazy. They were capable of other conversations sure, he'd heard them, rambling on about one thing or the other, but this, they always came back to this—scratching in the god-damn dirt. He hated these hens.

He lunged up behind them. "Pretty chickens," he hissed through his teeth. "You know the man's going to slaughter you, don't you? Don't you know? Slaughter us and eat us?" He was crying. "Slaughter us and eat us, slaughter us and eat us."

The young rooster flung him into the dirt. The old rooster kept his eyes closed. The young rooster lifted him off the ground and brushed off his feathers. One of the hens came over and held her face very close to his. "Knock it off," she said.

The rooster swallowed. He turned his back on them, scrambled back inside to his perch. He gripped it with his feet and stared out through the wire at the grassy valley and the farmhouse. Clouds changed their shapes slowly in the sky, rotating.

He could hear the hens.

"I've been reflecting on the nature of the self," one hen said to another. The rooster wondered if he'd heard this correctly. What did that hen just say? He turned his head to see. The other hen nodded slowly.

"Tricky, no?" she said.

The first hen nodded. They scratched contemplatively in the dirt. From his perch, the rooster craned his neck forward in confusion and listened.

"Am I who-I-was-yesterday? Am I not-who-I-was-yesterday?" The first hen's voice was quiet, probing. "This type of thing."

"How far down does it go, in other words," said the second hen. The rooster still couldn't tell if he was hearing correctly.

"I suppose that's it," agreed the first one. "How far down, if there is a down, and so on."

The hens were silent.

"I sometimes frame it in terms of karmic debt," said the second hen after a time.

"Interesting," said the first. "Go on."

"Well, relations of causality, you know. Action and consequence, lasting many lifetimes." The rooster looked around the coop in disbelief. Everything was the same as always—the chickens, the sky. He left his perch to keep listening.

"That's tricky as well," said the first hen.

"You don't have to tell me."

"Awkward for a Western mind to accept."

"Sure."

They scratched in the dirt.

"One question leads to another, doesn't it?" said the first hen.

The second hen made a noise of agreement.

"I guess what it might come down to for me," said the second hen after a while, "is deciding . . ." The rooster couldn't hear what she said next. It was something about "fundamentally"—did she say "until?" He moved even closer.

They were silent.

"Is it a white zebra with black stripes or a black zebra with white stripes, this type of thing?" the first hen asked.

The second hen laughed. "I suppose so. Has to do with emphasis."

"Figure and ground."

"Sure."

"Makes a difference, doesn't it?" They laughed together.

"Oh boy."

This entire exchange rattled the rooster deeply. He didn't know what it was about, it messed with him. His heart was racing. He considered knocking the hens down and pecking them, or stalking behind them hissing. He remembered the way the young rooster had lifted him up and brushed off his feathers. He went back inside and sat on the perch.

He came outside again. He pecked at the ground, worked his way back over toward the hens. Something was happening between the hens that he wanted to hear. He'd never known that the hens talked like that. What else would the hens say? He wanted very badly to keep listening to the hens talk.

"Well put," one of the hens was saying as the rooster approached. They were silent then for a while.

"Are you hungry?" asked the first hen, and for the first time the rooster seemed to understand that by this she meant something else, something more than the question.

"Yes, I am," said the second hen and again the rooster seemed to understand that what she meant by this was somehow below the words, or despite the words, like a code or another language. The rooster seemed to understand that the hens' conversation wasn't about their hunger and their plans at all. Or else it was about their hunger and their plans but in some way he had never considered, or considered so long ago that he could no longer remember it.

"Well, let's scratch in the dirt," said the first hen.

"Yes, let's scratch in the dirt," said the second hen.

The two hens scratched in the dirt, finding tiny left-over kernels of feed, which they gulped down. The rooster wished they would keep talking. Tentatively, he drew even nearer.

"Are you thirsty?" asked the first hen.

"I am," said the second hen.

"Let's drink water."

"Yes, let's drink water."

The hens drank water in great gulps.

The rooster's head was spinning. The way that the hens were talking to each other was like nothing he had ever imagined. Were they saying what they meant? Did they mean something more or something less than they were saying? He was wildly confused. He had the feeling of being in a dream, a migraine-blur to his vision. That night, he slept unsteadily and woke early.

The next day, again he listened while the hens talked.

"One does what one can, is that the idea?"

"Inherited tools."

"To put into words that wordlessness. Or pre-wordness, you could call it."

"Hmm."

"Because without trying to . . ."

"It's just an admission of failure, right?"

"Although even that failure . . ." The first hen trailed off. The second hen was silent for a while.

"Sure. I see."

They stood together without speaking.

"Wow," said the second hen.

They scratched in the dirt.

"Are you hungry?" asked the second hen and the rooster seemed to understand that by this she meant, "I'm hungry," or "would you like to share my hunger?"

"Yes, I am," the first hen said, and the rooster seemed to understand that by this she meant, "I'm glad that you're hungry," or "let's scratch in the dirt."

"Let's scratch in the dirt," said the second hen.

"Yes, let's scratch in the dirt."

The rooster walked around the coop in circles. He didn't know what to do, how to hold his body. The sun shone on the coop, on the hens and the young rooster. They clucked and pecked and strutted around and the old rooster wondered what else he didn't understand about the way these chickens talked to each other, about who these chickens were. He tried for a moment to imagine himself as a young rooster, to imagine the young rooster's life. He remembered the feeling of strong legs and wings, how it felt to flap and strut. He remembered eating in the sunshine, and cool water. He remembered when he used to crow in the mornings.

He thought about the hens. He wondered where they had come from. It had never occurred to him before to wonder. Had they been loaded in a truck? Had the journey been frightening? Did they remember their old home? He stared at the young rooster, stared at the chickens, and as he stared he seemed to feel a line dividing him from them. Not a line, precisely. A gap. A distinction. He looked at that distinction, focused on it, and somehow as he held it in his mind, as he looked at it, it seemed to him that he could rotate that distinction, could make it turn. He could make it wider or thinner, could stand it on its side. This was all in his mind, he understood this, it was something he was able to imagine doing. He imagined turning the distinction from side to side, and then he imagined making it begin to dissolve. It was a trick of the mind, a story. He watched the line—the gap, distinction—between himself and the young rooster begin to thin and blur, and he seemed for a moment to become the young rooster, to be standing on young legs in the middle of the coop, looking through the wire toward the house. And he let the distinction keep blurring, imagined that the line would keep blurring and it seemed to him now that he became one of the hens, and then another one, and he seemed to feel the colors of their minds, the blues and greens and reds, seemed to feel those colors washing in his own mind, behind his own old rooster eyes.

He shook himself. He stalked in confusion around the coop, went inside and sat on the perch. The hens were talking, and again, he drew nearer to listen. The sun felt warm on his feathers.

"Are you thirsty?" asked one hen, and the rooster seemed to understand that by this she meant, "you are thirsty," or "I love that you're thirsty," or "I love our thirst." He seemed to feel the colors of the hen's mind inside his own mind.

"Yes, I am," said the other hen, and the rooster seemed to understand that by this she meant, "I love your thirst," or "my thirst loves you," or "my thirst loves us."

"I am the thirst that loves the thirst you are," the rooster whispered to himself, though he had no idea what he meant. "I thirst for the love I have for our thirst," he said.

"Let's drink water," said the hen.

"Yes, let's drink water."

The rooster again stalked in circles around the coop. Again, looking at the hens and the young rooster, he imagined a line dividing them, or a gap, and again he imagined letting the gap dissolve until he could imagine the life of the young rooster, and imagine the lives of the hens, and feel the colors inside their minds with his own mind, and then he kept going, kept letting the gap dissolve—looking around at the beautiful coop—and he remembered the man inside the house and he let the gap or the line or whatever it was keep dissolving until it seemed to him that he could dimly imagine the life of the man inside the house, and he imagined then the life of the woman inside the house and it was as if he were the young rooster and were the hens and were the man and the woman inside the house, and he kept on going, letting the line dissolve and he remembered the fox.

The old rooster, the rooster in the thorns, he stood in the middle of the coop and he remembered the fox and he let the line keep dissolving, dissolve until it was gone—how much courage did it take to let that line dissolve?—and then he seemed to become the fox, he was crying now in great gasps, his small chest shaking violently. He was a fox, feeling the fur on his back, his tail in the air, the way his paws picked delicately through the mud. The sobs tore through rooster who was a fox, the rooster imagining himself a fox, and he let the sobs come, cried until there was no rooster anymore, and no fox, there was only crying, only grief, at the memories of those awful things—the way the fox devoured those hens, hens the rooster had known, hens he hadn't really known and now would never be able to know, miraculous, unique, once-in-a-lifetime hens, devoured. By a fox, while he watched. By the fox he was now able to imagine himself being. By the fox he now was. Those memories of the awful things the fox had done. And also—all mixed together, it was only one memory now, the same way it was only one grief—the memory of the things the rooster had done. He had sneaked out of the coop without warning those miraculous hens, those hens, and they had been torn to pieces because of him. They had endured great fear and pain because of his actions. He remembered how the thorns ripped his feathers. He remembered how the fox ripped the hens, and he was in that moment both the hens and the fox and himself, that younger self, that rooster, huddled in the rain and the thorns, terrified and mute.

The other chickens in the coop had gathered around the weeping, thrashing rooster. He stood and lurched toward one of the hens. "Are you hungry?" he heard himself say, by which he meant, "help."

The hen looked shocked. "What?" she asked.

"Please," he said, by which he meant, "please." "Are you hungry?" he asked again.

The hen was silent, she was backing away from him, she was shaking her head. The rooster thought his body would collapse again into the dirt. One of the other hens stepped forward. She turned her head sideways, looked at him carefully. It was the hen who had told him to knock it off when the young rooster had brushed off his feathers. They looked at each other.

"Yes," the hen said.

The rooster couldn't believe it, he didn't know what to think. He understood that the hen meant something he didn't understand. He wanted to understand what the hen had meant by that yes.

"Let's scratch in the dirt," he said, by which he meant, "I want to understand what you meant when you said yes."

"Yes, let's scratch in the dirt," she replied and he still didn't know what she meant.

They scratched together in the dirt for a time, and the other chickens scratched with them, and the rooster let the line dividing him from them and from the man and the woman and the fox dissolve completely, until there was only one scratching, only one dirt, and he raised himself up and he looked around, up at the sky, back down at the ground, at his own miraculous red rooster legs, and he crowed—like the first rooster on earth, like the inventor of crowing, like the inventor of roosters and chickens and foxes, he crowed, it's what roosters do, they crow—and the hens and the young rooster, they stood in a loose circle around him, and they listened, and they scratched in the dirt for their food.

FOUR

I WAS DIGGING A HOLE

I was digging a hole to bury my regrets in: that I have spoken
harshly to those I love, that I am distant and frightened and
self-involved. It was going to be a pretty deep hole. My palms
ached from the shovel's rough handle.

Foolish thoughts, foolish words, foolish actions: all
headed in there. That was the plan at least. Moonlight and
crickets. I was aware of my exhaustion, frayed nerves.

I'm kind of in a messed-up spot, I said out loud, and I heard
a voice (it was my voice) say "Compared to what?"—and the
ground lurched.

Paused.

There is no *baseline* spot in relationship to which any
other spot can be described as *kind of messed up.*

The earth slid from the shovel . . . the shovel from my
hands . . .

Is this how the kite feels when the string snaps?

The moonlight filled the hole and came boiling over the edges like milk.

HAPPY FOR NO REASON

Gunshots two in a row, pop pop, and then a car horn. Long sounding of a car horn. It goes on. A drawn-out moan. Or howl, maybe. Or wail. How do you describe a car horn? I don't know, I was a kid. For half an hour or more, it sounded and sounded, and finally the ambulance came.

The siren got louder, covering the noise of the horn, hiding it, then the siren stopped and there was just the horn again. Flat line of sound. Doors slammed, voices of the paramedics. A minute or two later—finally, finally—the horn stopped.

Let me try again. The sound of the gun was like this: pop pop, and then the car horn, a sustained note made of metal, going on and on and on. It took a while for me to understand. The sirens and the voices of the paramedics in the street. I stayed awake for a long time. I was probably ten years old and I was scared.

I lied to my dad at breakfast the next morning. He and my mom had been talking in hushed voices. I could feel the closeness between them. They were getting ready to go to work. He leaned forward carefully, asked if I had heard the commotion. I said no.

"You really didn't hear anything?" He was staring at me over his coffee cup. His eyes were sweet and tired.

"No, not at all," I said. After a second, he looked away.

He is my father and he loves me.

His thin mouth. He touched my cheek with a knuckle. I used to dangle my entire body from one of his arms. The kitchen was warm, steam on the windows.

He laughed a little. "I swear," he told me, "sometimes you sleep like the dead."

SIMPLE

A young man, a student of biology, decides to try to call Nora Gutierrez. That's wise of him, calling, practical, there are precautions worth taking, so he manages to find a working payphone and he looks in the directory, and who knows if the woman he's looking for is listed, or if she even has a phone, he hurls coin after coin into the slot, describes what he saw, quickly, three sentences at the most, hangs up. Dials, speaks, hangs up. If it's not the right woman on the other end, maybe it's a cousin, or a neighbor with the same name. The student doesn't know, he never signed up for this saint job, it's something, at least he called, most people wouldn't even have called, he runs out of coins after eleven names. In a few years, he'll earn his degree, work briefly in a bank, which he won't like, go back to his studies, put himself through school by working part-time as an auto mechanic, eventually join the university's faculty. He'll get married, have one child, a boy with wispy hair and a thick nose, a boy who walks around sometimes on his hands. He'll get divorced. Always, he'll like red wine, accordion music, trout fishing. He'll never take the backpacking trip through Patagonia he sometimes thinks about. He'll never grow the long beard he threatens to. Mornings he will sleep late if he can. His laugh will be a little too loud, always, off-putting, forced—it's a bray, his laugh, mouth open. He has called eleven people, and maybe the twelfth would've been the right one, he'll never know. He pushes himself away from the phone and walks down the street, so much motion, newspapers and magazines for sale, traffic, pigeons in the sunshine, something catches in his chest, people at sidewalk tables drinking coffee, laughing, arguing, waving their hands around, maybe the twelfth call would've been the right one, he won't ever know, he just won't, so what, he doesn't care, tells himself he doesn't care, and anyway, a thing like that—picking up his stride, heading toward the corner, toward the rest of his life—who would *want* to know?

THE DEVIL'S NEW RED AXE

One summer day the devil appeared to a simple woodcutter and offered him a new red axe. The woodcutter, dazzled, accepted the axe, which was lighter and sharper than any he had ever seen. That morning, he chopped and stacked over a week's worth of wood; that afternoon he chopped and stacked even more.

His sons eyed each other carefully.

His wife brought her hand to her mouth.

At the tiniest motion of his wrist, the axe lashed out. A few minutes and the thickest trunk crashed to earth. The man shouted with joy.

Behind him, the devil was turning his wife into a poplar, and his sons—his three beautiful sons—into pines.

THE SAVANNAH

Do you remember? You were there, and I was there, and the others. We groomed each other's fur. All the time I was scared, of those noises in the dark, of the wide sky. I touched my face with my hand.

Someone ran screeching through the valley, galloping on feet and fists. We laughed. I had fleas, constantly—constantly. They swarmed over me.

Do you remember how it was? My memories keep shifting. Today, though, when I was sitting at the bus stop and you drove by in your baby blue Mustang with the top down, I recognized you, I think. Am I getting this right? I was the one who tossed twig after twig into the river where they floated away? And you were the smaller one who banged together the round stones?

THE DONKEY AT THE GATES OF
THE KINGDOM OF HEAVEN

Once a donkey ascended to the shining gates of the kingdom of heaven. The gates were open. The donkey heard music more beautiful than anything he had ever imagined. Each note was a star going supernova, a pack of wolves running down an elk over snow. The song poured itself into the world. The donkey stood transfixed. Without thinking, he opened his mouth wide and brayed.

Instantly the music stopped.

Total silence.

His bray had been off-key, awful. A donkey's sound.

Slowly, the gates of the kingdom of heaven began to swing shut. The donkey didn't know what to do, whether he should advance or retreat. The light was blinding. He took one trembling step forward, then another. He couldn't see a thing.

The donkey brayed again, knowing it would not be beautiful. He was right; it wasn't beautiful. It was his same old donkey bray. He did it again and again. He couldn't tell if the gates were open now or closed, or even where they were exactly. He shut his eyes and thought about the entirety of his life. He remembered eating hay, carrying firewood.

He brayed again. He did. He let it rip. He kept his eyes closed and staggered forward, belting it out. Carrier of firewood, eater of hay. He took his whole life's only song and he employed it—step after step into brightness, into terrible dazzling light.

SIMPLE

Buenos Aires, 1979

Wilson Ramón Gutierrez

b. 1960

FIVE

THE BABY

The baby's by itself on a blanket. Expanse of grass, expanse of gray sky. The man flinches, and the flinch becomes a little shiver, a shiver of disgust almost. He stops walking. Baby on a blanket in a tiny park.

The man had been picking his exhausted, miserable way back to the car from the hospital, but now this: the baby turns its head. On the blanket are a few toys.

The man looks behind him on the sidewalk, across the street, but sees no other pedestrians. Cars thrum by along the avenue toward the hospital entrance and the highway on the other side. Gray day, breezy, clouds thickening. The man's name is William Harper, although everyone calls him Billy; he is a white man with dark eyes and thinning hair; and six days ago he was told that he has stage four prostate cancer, metastases to liver and bone. Each step, he moves around himself, around that tender central part of himself where legs and torso join. He oscillates between weepiness and hot, ludicrous rage. He can't find a comfortable angle at which to hold his arms.

The baby makes a sound, a sort of coughing sound, a little hack, and it gives a tentative cry, orienting its body toward Billy, face mashing up, the pacifier dropping from its mouth to the blanket. Billy turns one full circle, looking in all directions, but sees only the cars on their oblivious way. When his daughters were babies, he would chew at their cheeks, fake-snarling, gum at them, and the girls would squeal in delight. His daughters: Jennifer, Rose.

The baby stiffens its little body, throws its head back, punches both arms and shouts once, mouth open. The mouth seems too large for the head somehow, out of proportion. For a moment, Billy sees the baby's tongue, and then the baby takes a breath, shouts again, pitch rising, the face reddening, and Billy hesitates, unsure—a long moment—before he steps onto the grass toward the baby, of course he does, what's he going to do, keep walking? Go to the car? A volunteer from the Cancer Society had called to offer him a ride and he'd never called her back. He feels dizzy, nauseous. This morning the oncologist had said something about "quality of life." Once they start talking about quality of life, Billy had thought, reeling, gripping his hands together in his lap, trying not to scream or to sob, well, that sure tells you a lot. He didn't really hear anything else the oncologist said.

The baby's cries are like a bandsaw.

When Jennifer, when Rose, kicked and wailed. When they wanted. When they hurt, when they raged. All those years of getting out of bed at their call, swinging his feet to the floor and standing before he was even fully awake, of working weekends to pay for the nanny and the piano lessons and the braces and the vacations in Hawaii. Since he left their mom, they've changed with him, his daughters, closed ranks. The women of his family, shoulder to shoulder. Women now.

With a rush of shame, he kneels painfully down at the edge of the blanket, makes a hello-sound, tries to smile. The blanket alternates dark- and light-green stripes. The baby's shriek lasts impossibly long, then a gasp for air, then again: poor terrible little animal. It's wearing a brown onesie with a giraffe on it. Hard to tell if it's a boy or a girl, even this close. Round red face, wisps of hair, mouth all the way open. No teeth.

"Hey hey hey," he says, wiggling his fingers, reaching for the child.

"Hey hey hey," patting the soft side of the body. The baby writhes on its back, screaming.

On the blanket there's a stuffed snail and a plastic contraption: a ball within a framework of plastic honeycombing parts. He's seen them before. When you pick it up, it rattles. He picks it up with his non-patting hand and it rattles.

"Hey hey hey," rattling. The baby cries out, stops for a huge gulp of air, shouts again. There are so many kinds of cries—he remembers now. He feels tears in a sudden rush behind his eyes and curses, shudders, grunts the tears away. He has yet to tell his family of his diagnosis, to tell anyone at all. The facts don't fit anywhere into the shape of his life. There's no room for them, no angle at which they can enter. How can a person talk about something like that? There isn't a way.

"Hey hey hey."

This baby has eyelashes, dozens of them in a row. This baby has giant brown eyes, tears on the sides of its red cheeks. It cries out at the situation in which it finds itself, alone on a blanket in a park. Its cries heave up, using the entire little body. Its arms and legs kick out in fury. Billy is trying to remember the songs. There was one about a bus.

He is still fighting his own tears, his helpless, overwhelming guilt. "The itsy bitsy spider," he croaks, but the key's wrong, coughs, starts again. "The itsy-bitsy spider." There were hand gestures, too, weren't there, that went with it? He keeps rattling the ball. "Went up the water spout." The baby thrashes, howls.

And his pride in them. Oh God, the pride. It was uncontainable. At their sassiness, their opinions. The way they crawled, walked, strutted, these daughters, Jennifer nine years old shooting baskets in the driveway, shouting "boom" at each swish. When he left, he left in an eruption. "Your mom and I used to like each other," he told Rose, trying to explain. Hearing the bitterness in his own words, hearing his own cynicism. How could he possibly explain? "But now we just don't." Which was true.

"And down came the rain and *washed* the spider out."

A long breath now, a whimper, a new sound. The song retains its magical powers, even after all these years; he animates his face, widens his eyes, minces the words, "up came the sun and dried out all the rain." Is it dried *out* or dried *up*? Rose's bicycle, Rose's braces, Rosie slamming the door. He left, he left, he left for someone else, her name was Amanda, for the way he felt alive with her, *embodied,* and she turned around and left him less than three months later and the symmetrical devastating irony of it lodged in his groin and turned right into cancer and now it's going to kill him. He should have never gone near his body, the alive and roaring feeling of his middle-aged body. His body wants to murder him. His body wants to burn him up, disappear him. He feels dizzy. His mouth tastes sour.

"And the itsy bitsy spider *went up the spout again.*"

The baby continues to whimper, but it's interested, changing registers. "It went up the spout," Billy hears himself cry out again—the repeated ending he always added with his own kids. "What did it want up there?" The baby makes a sound that's more like a coo, a little gasp-coo, and the man reaches a hand to touch the side of the baby's face. It's warm, firm, flushed. He puts down the rattly toy and picks up the pacifier, presents it solemnly to the baby, who grasps it in its own little hand, then brings it to its mouth in a rush and begins to slurp.

"Yeah," he says.

"That's right," he says. He feels now an incredible tenderness, looking at this baby, and the tenderness reminds him of the unacceptability of this situation—of a baby left by itself on a blanket in a park—and he rises to his knees to look around. He is indignant on this baby's behalf. Who leaves a baby out in the world? Even if it's just to pee or something, who? There is no bathroom, though, no public bathroom in sight: maybe in one of the buildings of the hospital? He has a sudden image of himself confronting a parent, some dopey young mother in baggy clothes and a vague hippy manner. He imagines himself poking a finger in her face.

The baby takes the pacifier out of its mouth and waves it around in the air. After a snort, it begins again to cry.

Billy scoops the baby up, stands with a long grunt: a heaving awkward squat his body remembers, how one of the girls'd drop a pacifier while he walked them back and forth and he'd have to crouch down to pick it up without tipping her out of her precise balance in the crook of his arm. The baby is still sobbing. He moves the head into the curve of his neck, encourages a pillowing, a safety. "The itsy bitsy spider," he starts again. The warm little body kicks against his and he hears the song he's singing, really hears it: that spider didn't quit. Washed down, climbed up, forever. A hot rush in his throat. That spider didn't let them get away with it.

The cries modulate one more time, shift a key. He'd forgotten how complicated the sounds were, and how loud, the long songs of crashing emotion, their ups and downs, the operatic, overwhelming noise. The kid's right in his ear. The pacifier is back on the ground again somehow, and again he squats, tips over just a hair before he rebalances and stands. He's lost his place, starts over. "The itsy, bitsy spider." He smells shit in the diaper and again looks around. No one. "Went up the water spout." He could change the diaper, he thinks, and suddenly he wants to: wants to know if this is a boy or a girl; it matters, matters a lot, it's knowledge he needs, knowledge that changes the whole situation one way or another. Jennifer, Rose, his daughters.

The woman Amanda, the one that he left them all for, she was hilarious and reckless and drove too fast. She was fifteen years younger than him and she dyed her hair jet-black and the whole thing was over in a matter of months. There's a rage in him he can barely contain. "You're creeping me out," she'd told him, exasperated one night when he wouldn't leave her apartment in his shame and fury and lust, and he hadn't had a thing to say, not a word, staring at her, stunned, sweating.

He sways his body back and forth, eyeing the bag on the ground. With his foot, he tries to open it, look inside. If there are diapers in there, he thinks. He's humming now, tunelessly, a little out of breath, the song left behind, and his humming and the baby's shrieks are harmonizing, finding their relationship. The baby gives a little gasp, carries on. There are diapers in the bag, he can see them, and a plastic container of wipes. Again he looks around the empty park.

He is in an altered state. He has that realization. He recognizes that fact. The cancer, the queasy sky, his life in shambles, this stranger's child weeping in his arms.

He lays the baby down, gently, pillowing the head. The baby kicks its legs, squirms, the cries ramping up again. It bucks up against his hand, and he pushes harder, holding the baby down with his right hand while his left fumbles in the bag for a diaper and a bag of wipes. He is alive and this baby is alive, wrestling against him on this blanket, and he is going to change this baby so that it is clean and warm. He is going to identify if this is a son or a daughter and that fact will alter the meaning of this experience in some profound way. He wonders what gender he's hoping for, and he really can't tell. The baby flings the pacifier away. Billy starts to sob.

Through his tears he scoops up the pacifier, holds it out again to the baby who grabs for it and pulls it desperately to its mouth. Sucking, its eyes soften and it takes a deep breath.

"That's right," Billy says. He is on his knees. He pats the baby's side. He pulls the little socks off, slides the pants down. Those feet are pudgy and small. They are the feet of a living baby, of a person with a future. Billy's tears stop as abruptly as they began.

The diaper has tabs that pull open. He pulls the tabs open. The baby eyes him in an interested fashion around the pacifier. Billy Harper opens the diaper and gently, gently cleans the shit off the little boy's penis and thighs, folding each wipe and tossing it aside, lifting the boy's ankles to wipe the buttocks, cleaning under and around the scrotum with great care.

The boy is in his lap, diaper changed, onesie back on. They are sitting together on a blanket in the park. The boy has the pacifier in a tight fist. I haven't had a good life, Billy thinks, I haven't been happy, and almost instantly he changes his mind. That's not right, that's not right at all. Even if it had been a better life, a good life, a perfect life: it still wouldn't have been enough, it wouldn't have been enough. No life is enough. And it was a good life anyway, wasn't it, in its own way? Good and bad aren't the relevant categories. Not enough isn't a relevant category. What are the relevant categories? He can't find them anywhere. The baby murmurs and moves.

When Billy was a young man, his first year in college, he remembers a pool table on a lower level in his dormitory, and a heavyset older guy who used to shoot the balls slowly, glacially—they'd roll and kiss against each other and drop precisely into the pockets—and he thought that was so cool, so beautiful, the skill of it, and the confidence. The guy shot once, and chalked his cue, and moved slowly, formally, around the table to shoot again. It was gorgeous.

Earlier in the week, he had gone to have coffee with Rose in her new apartment, and she'd been stiff with him and wounded and closed-off and he hadn't known how to even begin to share his news. "Classes are good?" he had asked, and she had talked about econ and about her poetry workshop, and he had let her talk, let her talk, nodding.

"So I went to the doctor," he could've said. Outside her third floor window, a squirrel ran on a bare branch, paused, continued. Rose's fingernails were painted dark blue. She picked her phone up from the table, turned it over in her hands, placed it back down. The words were there in his throat, thick, viscous.

"I remember the day you were born," he could've said. Just blurted it out. He was so exhausted. He was so brittle and exhausted and overwhelmed, sitting with his beautiful hurt daughter, the whole universe tilting and veering. "I remember your entire life," he could've said.

The squirrel darted down the trunk and disappeared.

"Sweetheart," he could've begun, and then just said whatever came out next. But he hadn't. He'd known his voice would break, could feel it in his throat, right there.

Rose had affected surprise when she looked at her phone for the time. "God, Dad," she'd said.

"Oh," he said, and swallowed. "Sure."

She wasn't looking at him. "You know," she said.

"Sure," he said again.

"I'm so sorry," she said, standing.

There were other songs, too, Billy thinks now, weren't there? He can't remember any of them. The baby's skin is so soft. The baby's eyes are alert. Billy looks hard at the baby's face, and as he looks the face seems to shift in some fashion, to reconstitute itself within his gaze, and Billy has the feeling that he is looking at the face of an old man, a tiny old man, no teeth. It's a funny feeling, a reversal. Billy is older than this baby, but this old man is older than Billy, and Billy wonders if there's an old man inside his face that is even older than the old man staring at him from inside the baby, and he almost sees, or almost feels, the succession of old men in each of them. His father is there, and his grandfather, and the father and grandfather of the baby.

"Hi," he says, to the old men in the baby, and the baby murmurs something that he takes to be the old men in the baby returning the greeting to the old men in him, the long line.

The old men in him look at the old men in this baby, and at the very young man the baby is. Not just any old men, Billy reminds himself suddenly: old men with cancer, and the succession of old men that are Billy Harper, of men of all ages that are Billy Harper, look from within their cancerous bodies at the cancer-free body of the baby and the cancer-free men of different ages in the baby, but that isn't right either. It's just cancer of different ages. This baby is an early version of something like Billy Harper, just as Billy Harper is an older version of something like this baby—so the cancer in him is just a later version of the cancer-pattern in this baby, the latent cancer, the cancer not yet developed. The series of men in him greet the series of men in the baby, and the cancers in him, the succession of various cancers in him, greet the cancers in the baby.

Cancer is just a pattern, too, isn't it? A particular organization of cells. From within his body, to the older cancers of the older men within his body, does the cancer swelling in him feel like a baby? A baby cancer.

A mother and father cancer, and a baby cancer. They go for a walk. Or two baby cancers, maybe, two baby girl cancers. God, Dad, one of the daughter cancers says, looking at her phone, I'm so sorry, and the father nods, swallows. The mother and father, their life together—it's just patterns, he thinks.

Something in him thinks, it's just patterns, and all the different men of different ages, and the women too, the women of different ages, his daughters there, and his mother and grandmothers, his aunts and unknown great-aunts and all the different cancers that each of them carries inside, or might carry inside, past and present and future twining around each other, all of them think it too, simultaneously, it's just patterns. The baby moves in his arms.

The cancer family. They made a life. They came together and they came apart, and that's all cancer itself is, when you get down to it, cells coming together and coming apart. Like pool balls, billiard balls, slowly clicking against each other and rolling apart. A guy from college chalked his cue with an easy gesture and moved around the table and a dozen other guys of other ages within that guy moved with him, and a hundred cancers moved along as well, chalking their cues.

The father and the mother. They met at a dance. They were introduced by friends. The mother had long, straight hair; she wore a flowered dress. Her name was Emily. She carried a succession of young and old women inside of her, all wearing that flowered dress. The band played "Bridge Over Troubled Water." It must have been thousands of flowered dresses.

Thousands of men of different ages and thousands of cancers inside of them stand and move across thousands of dance floors to thousands of women and cancers, and they dance, all of them, the whole crowd. The scale of everything is different now. Even this baby. Even this baby is dancing, the cells inside him moving in patterns that organize themselves into older babies, into toddlers and young men and adults and old men, or into cancers and more cancers. This baby dances by moving its hands, making a noise that sounds like "oh." "Oh," this baby says.

This baby has the face of Billy Harper's mother and father, and of Billy Harper's grandparents. It's clear as day. It's hard to believe he hadn't seen it before, this baby with his ancestors' faces within its face, the cancer baby there wearing the faces of the cancer ancestors, all the way back. Cancer with the ancestors' one face, rearranging itself into each particular face down the line through the generations, patterns that shift and rotate, that do what we want or don't do what we want.

"What do we want?" old chant, call-and-response—a young man turns and asks an older man, inside of Billy Harper, "What do we want?" and simultaneously the mouths move of all the other men, of all the generations, each of them asking, "What do we want?"

The father turns to the mother on a dance floor, and he asks her "What do we want?" and as he moves his mouth, the generations of other men and other cancers move their mouths and ask the generations of other women and other cancers, "What do we want?" A roar of voices, and all of the women and the cancers answer with their own roar, "What do we want?" Patterns of mouths moving. Mouths that are themselves patterns moving in patterns, "What do we want?" A bird flies up from a tree, and as it flies it asks

"What do we want?" and it metastasizes into other birds, thousands of birds in thousands of trees, beaks and mouths asking, and then a woman stands up, one of the women in the flowered dress, a woman with the blood drained out of her face, Billy Harper's wife, his wife Emily, and she looks him squarely in the eyes and she asks, "What do *you* want, Billy?" Changing one word, shifting the emphasis, but not accusing, not angry, just stunned: stunned and empty and sad, changing the emphasis again, "Billy, what do you *want?*" Squeezing her hands together.

The middle-aged man and the baby are sitting on a green-striped blanket. The question hangs in the air between them and between the many men there in the baby and the babies in the man. It's a real question. It's the only question that matters. Everyone's waiting for an answer.

"Not this," Billy Harper says. He says it out loud. He says it with his mouth, but it isn't his answer, or not only his answer, it's the answer of the others as well, the answer of the men and the women, the parents, the daughters, the babies, the cancers. It's the answer of the pattern itself. "Not this," says the pattern itself.

"God, Dad," one of the cancer daughters says to the cancer father, looking at her phone, and the father stands and says, "Not this." "Not this," he says, and the daughter opens her mouth wide, thousands of daughters open their mouths wide, "Not this." Women calling out to women, men to men, cancers to cancers, "Not this." The birds crying to each other in a thousand skies, the babies shrieking on a thousand blankets in a thousand empty parks, "Not this."

Anything but this.

A young woman stands from a baby on a blanket. The baby is wearing a brown onesie with a giraffe on it; he moves his hands and says "oh." She hears him say "oh" and she turns and starts to run and inside of her is a terrible hot roar, a hurricane swirl with no let-up, women of all ages inside of her watching helplessly and waving their arms: she is leaving her baby in a park.

Her life has come to a place where it has required her—to where she thinks it has required her, to where it seems to her that her life has required her—to leave her baby in a park. Billy can see her life require this of her, can see her turn and start to run. It's all happening in front of him, somehow, right where he can see it: the woman running, the women inside of her waving their arms, the baby lying on the blanket, blinking at the sky.

"Oh honey," Billy calls, calls after her and the women inside of her who are waving their arms and themselves calling after her. The men inside of Billy joined now by the women inside of Billy, the babies, the cancers, all joining their voices to the voices inside of the running woman, the babies left on blankets inside of the running woman. "Oh honey," he calls, they all call together, the whole crowd calling, pleading, the woman his daughter's age maybe, his own daughter. "Oh honey," they call. "Please not this."

Cancers calling, babies calling, birds and cancers and babies calling, "Not this." If he could just catch up to her, he thinks, they think, the men and women and cancers think, they all think together, if they could just catch up to her, but they can't: it is too late.

Billy Harper understands her perfectly.

"Oh honey, no," he tries again, but she is already gone.

ACKNOWLEDGMENTS

A profound thank you to the editors of the publications where these pieces first appeared, often in substantially different versions.

Alaska Quarterly Review: "The New Bear"

American Literary Review: "The Rooster in the Thorns"

Forklift, Ohio: "Thomas Jefferson," "Poor, Lonely Donkey," "Plan A/Plan B," "Most of us around here," "The Exact Thing," "Memorial"

Glossolalia: "The Emperor's Swans," "The Tigerkeeper's Daughter" (under the title "The Tigerkeeper")

Hanging Loose: "Simple"

Kenyon Review Online: "The Devil's New Red Axe," The Savannah," "The Baby"

The Massachusetts Review: "Boom-Boom Whoop"

Puerto del Sol: "Every life is a private life," "Happy for no reason"

RHINO: "The Royal Butcher"

Salt Hill: "Lesson"

The Southeast Review: "Teaching," "Neighbors"

Spork: "Story"

The Sun: "Sobriety," "The Donkey at the Gates of the Kingdom of Heaven," "The Hogs, The Sow, The Wind"

Waxwing: "Fatherhood," "The Guest," "Employee," "A Method for Appeasing Jackals," "I was digging a hole," "Tree, Bird, Spoon"

Witness: "The Squirrels"

I've been the recipient of so much kindness and encouragement and support. It can't be measured. I've tried. It really can't.

Grateful thanks to Amy Parker, Daniel Herman, Bryan Clark, Rebeccah Miller, Emily Buchanan, Shauna Hannibal, Teresa Poore, Erin Stalcup, Justin Bigos, Colleen Donfield, Andrew Snee, Derek Askey, Sy Safranksy, Mary Jane Nealon, Joseph Scapellato, Lynette D'Amico, Amy Wright, Kevin Brockmeier, Nate Pritts, Tricia Suit and Eric Appleby.

Kevin McIlvoy and Matt Hart: joyful engines.

Gaelyn Godwin: Zen ocean.

Marj Byler, David H. Rutschman, Jiryu Mark Rutschman-Byler: from the beginning.

And Devon, Ella, Leo: always, always, and for everything.

May all beings be happy and free from suffering.

ABOUT THE AUTHOR

David Rutschman is a Soto Zen priest
and hospice grief counselor. His work has
appeared in *Forklift, Ohio*; *Kenyon Review
Online*; *The Massachusetts Review*; *The Sun*;
Waxwing; *Witness*; and elsewhere. He lives
in California with his wife and two young
children. This is his first book.

Made in the USA
San Bernardino, CA
27 January 2018